The Adventures of Martin Hewitt by Arthur Morrison

Arthur Morrison was born on November 1st, 1863, in Poplar, in the East End of London. From the age of 8, after the death of his father, he was brought up, along with two siblings, by his mother, Jane.

Morrison spent his youth in the East End. In 1879 he began as an office boy in the Architect's Department of the London School Board and, in his spare time, visited used bookstores in Whitechapel Road. He first published, a humorous poem, in the magazine Cycling in 1880.

In 1885 Morrison began writing for The Globe newspaper. In 1886, he switched to the People's Palace, in Mile End and, in 1888, published the Cockney Corner collection, about life in Soho, Whitechapel, Bow Street and other areas of London.

By 1889 he was an editor at the Palace Journal, reprinting some earlier sketches, and writing commentaries on books and articles on the life of the London poor.

By 1890 he was back at The Globe and published 'The Shadows Around Us', a supernatural collection of stories. Also at this time he began to develop a keen interest in Japanese Art.

In October 1891 his short story A Street appeared in Macmillan's Magazine. The following year he married Elizabeth Thatcher and then befriended publisher and poet William Ernest Henley for whom he wrote stories of working-class life in Henley's National Observer between 1892-94.

In 1894 came his first detective story featuring Martin Hewitt, described as "a low-key, realistic, lower-class answer to Sherlock Holmes".

Morrison published A Child of the Jago in 1896 swiftly followed by The Adventures of Martin Hewitt.

In 1897 Morrison wrote seven stories about Horace Dorrington, a deeply corrupt private detective, described as "a cheerfully unrepentant sociopath who is willing to stoop to theft, blackmail, fraud or cold-blooded murder to make a dishonest penny."

To London Town, the final part of a trilogy including Tales of Mean Streets and A Child of the Jago was published in 1899. Following on came a wide spectrum of works, including novels, short stories and one act plays.

In 1911 he published his authoritative work Japanese Painters, illustrated with art from his own collection.

Although he retired from journalistic work in 1913 he continued to write about Art.

In his last decades Morrison served as a special constable, and reported on the first Zeppelin raid on London. Tragically in 1921 his son, Guy, who had survived the war, died of malaria.

The Royal Society of Literature elected him as a member in 1924 and to its Council in 1935.

In 1930 he moved to Chalfont St Peter, Buckinghamshire. Here he wrote the short story collection Fiddle o' Dreams and More.

Index of Contents

I. The Affair of Mrs. Seton's Child
II. The Case of Mr. Geldard's Elopement
III. The Case of the Dead Skipper
IV. The Case of the "Flitterbat Lancers"
V. The Case of the Late Mr. Rewse
VI. The Case of the Ward Lane Tabernacle
Arthur Morrison – A Concise Bibliography

I. — THE AFFAIR OF MRS. SETON'S CHILD

It has struck me that many of my readers may wonder that, although I have set down in detail a number of interesting cases wherein Hewitt figured with success, I have scarcely as much as alluded to his failures. For failures he had, and of a fair number. More than once he has found his search met, perhaps at the beginning, perhaps after some little while, by an impenetrable wall of darkness through which no clue led. At other times he has lost time on a false trail while his quarry escaped. At others still the stupidity or inaccuracy of some person upon whom he has depended for information has set his plans to naught. The reason why none of these cases have been embodied in the present papers is simply this; that a problem with no answer, a puzzle with no explanation, an incident with no satisfactory end, as a rule lends itself but poorly to purposes of popular narrative, and it is often difficult to make understood and appreciated any degree of skill and acumen unless it produces a clear and intelligible result. That such results attended Hewitt's efforts in an extraordinary degree those who have followed my narratives so far will need no assurance; but withal impossibilities still remain impossibilities, for Hewitt as for the dullest creature alive. On some other occasion I may perhaps set out at length a case in which Martin Hewitt achieved nothing more than unqualified failure; for the present I shall content myself with a case which, although it was completely cleared up in the end, yet for some while baffled Hewitt because of some of the reasons I have alluded to.

On the ground floor of the building wherein Hewitt kept his office, and in which I myself had my chambers, were the offices of Messrs. Streatley and Raikes, an old-fashioned firm of family solicitors. Messrs. Streatley and Raikes's junior clerk appeared in Hewitt's outer office one morning with the query, "Is your guv'nor in?"

Kerrett admitted the fact.

"Will you tell him Mr. Raikes sends his compliments and will be obliged if he can step downstairs for a few minutes? It's a client of ours—a lady—and she's in a great state about losing her baby or something. Say Mr. Raikes would bring her up only she seems too ill to get up the stairs."

This was the purport of the message which Kerrett brought into the inner room, and in three minutes Hewitt was in Streatley and Raikes's office.

"I thought the only useful thing possible would be to send for you, Mr Hewitt," Mr. Raikes explained; "indeed, if my client had been better acquainted with London no doubt she would have come to you direct. She is in a bad state in the inner office. Her name is Mrs. Seton; her husband is a recent client of ours. Quite young, and rather wealthy people, so far as I know. Made a fortune early, I believe, in South Africa, and calve here to live. Their child—their only child, a little toddler of two years or thereabout—disappeared yesterday in a most mysterious way, and all efforts to find it seem to have failed as yet. The police have been set going everywhere, but there is no news as yet. Mrs. Seton seems to have passed a dreadful night, and could think of nothing better to do this morning than to come to us. She has her maid with her, and looks to be breaking down entirely. I believe she's lying on the sofa in my private room now. Will you see her? I think you might hear what she has to say, whether you take the case in hand or not; something may strike you, and in any case it will comfort her to get your opinion. I told her all about you, you know, and she clutched at the chance eagerly. Shall I see if we may go in?"

Mr. Raikes knocked at the door of his inner sanctum and waited; then he knocked again and set the door ajar. There was a quiet "Come in," and pushing open the door the lawyer motioned Hewitt to follow him.

On the sofa facing the door sat a lady, very pale, and exhibiting plain signs of grief and physical weariness. A heavy veil was thrown back over her bonnet, and her maid stood at her side holding a bottle of salts. As she saw Hewitt she made as if to rise, but he stepped quickly forward and laid his hand on her shoulder. "Pray don't disturb yourself, Mrs. Seton," he said; "Mr. Raikes has told me something of your trouble, and perhaps when I know a little more I shall be able to offer you some advice. But remember that it will be very important for you to maintain your strength and spirits as much as possible."

"This is Mr. Martin Hewitt, you know," Mr. Raikes here put in—"of whom I was speaking."

Mrs. Seton inclined her head and with a very obvious effort began.

"It is my child, you know, Mr. Hewitt—my little boy Charley; we can't find him."

"Mr. Raikes has told me so. When did you see the child last?"

"Yesterday morning. His nurse left him sitting on the floor in a room we call the small morning-room, where we sometimes allowed him to play when nurse was out, because the nursery was out of hearing, except from the bedrooms. I myself was in the large morning-room, and as he seemed to be very quiet I went to look, and found he was not there."

"You looked elsewhere, of course?"

"Yes; but he was nowhere in the house, and none of the servants had seen him. At first I supposed that his nurse had gone back to the small morning-room and taken him with her—I had sent her on an errand—but when she returned I found that was not the case."

"Can he walk?"

"Oh, yes, he can walk quite well. But he could scarcely have come out from the room without my hearing him. The two rooms, the morning-room and the small sitting-room, are on opposite sides of the same passage."

"Do the doors face each other?"

"No; the door of the small room is farther up the passage than the other. But in any case he was nowhere in the house."

"But if he left the room he must have got out somehow. Is there no other door?"

"Yes, there is a French window, with the lower panels of wood, in the room; it gives on to a few steps leading down into the garden; but that was closed and bolted on the inside."

"You found no trace whatever of him, I take it, on the whole premises?"

"Not a trace of any sort, nor had anybody about the place seen him."

"Did you yourself actually see him in this room, or have you merely the nurse's word for it?"

"I saw her put him there. She left him playing with a box of toys. When if went to look for him the toys were there, scattered on the floor, but he had gone." Mrs. Seton sank on the arms of her maid and her breast heaved.

"I'm sure," Hewitt said, "You'll keep your nerves as steady as you can, Mrs. Seton; much may depend on it. If you have nothing else to tell me now I think I will come to your house at once, look at it, and question your servants myself. Meantime what has been done?"

"The police have been notified everywhere, of course," Mr. Raikes said, handing Hewitt a printed bill, damp from the press; "and here is a bill containing a description of the child and offering a reward, which is being circulated now."

Hewitt glanced at the bill and nodded. "That is quite right," he said, "so far as I can tell at present. But I must see the place. Do you feel strong enough to come home now, Mrs. Seton?"

Hewitt's business-like decision and confidence of manner gave the lady fresh strength. "The brougham is here," she said, "and we can drive home at once. We live at Cricklewood."

A fine pair of horses stood before the brougham, though they still bore signs of hard work; and indeed they had been kept at their best pace all that morning. All the way to Cricklewood Hewitt kept Mrs. Seton in conversation, never for a moment leaving her attention disengaged. The missing child, he learned, was the only one, and the family had only been in England for something less than a year. Mr. Seton had become possessed of real property in South Africa, had sold it in London, and had determined to settle here.

A little way past Shoot-up Hill the coachman swung his pair off to the left, and presently entering a gate pulled up before a large old-fashioned house.

Here Hewitt immediately began a complete examination of the premises. The possible exits from the grounds, he found, were four in number. The two wide front gates giving on to the carriage-drive, the kitchen and stable entrance, and a side gate in a fence—always locked, however. Inside the house, from the central hall, a passage to the right led to another wherein was the door of the small morning-room. This was a very ordinary room, 15 feet square or so, lighted by the glass in the French window, the bottom panes of which, however, had been filled in with wood. The contents of a box of toys lay scattered on the floor, and the box itself lay near.

"Have these toys been moved," Hewitt asked, "since the child was missed?"

"No, we haven't allowed anything to be disturbed. The disappearance seemed so wholly unaccountable that we thought the police might wish to examine the place exactly as it was. They did not seen to think it necessary, however."

Hewitt knelt and examined the toys without disturbing them. They were of very good quality, and represented a farmyard, with horses, carts, ducks, geese and cows complete. One of the carts had had a string attached so that it might be pulled along the floor.

"Now," Hewitt said rising, "you think, Mrs. Seton, that the child could not have toddled through the passage, and so into some other part of the house, without you hearing him?"

"Well," Mrs. Seton answered with indecision, "I thought so at first, but I begin to doubt. Because he must have done so, I suppose."

They went into the passage. The door of the large morning-room was four or five yards further toward the passage leading to the hall, and on the opposite side. "The floor in this passage," Hewitt observed, "is rather thickly carpeted. See here, I can walk on it at a good pace without noise."

Mrs. Seton assented. "Of course," she said, "if he got past here he might have got anywhere about the house, and so into the grounds. There is a veranda outside the drawing-room, and doors in various places.'

"Of course the grounds have been completely examined?"

"Oh, yes, every inch."

"The weather has been very dry, unfortunately," Hewitt said, "and it would be useless for me to look for footprints on your hard gravel, especially of so small a child. Let us come back to the room. Is the French window fastened as you found it?"

"Yes; nothing has been changed."

The French window was, as is usual, one of two casements joining in the centre and fastened by bolts top and bottom. "It is not your habit, I see," Hewitt observed, "to open both halves of the window."

"No; one side is always fastened, the other we secure by the bottom bolt because the catch of the handle doesn't always act properly."

"And you found that bolt fastened as I see it now?"

"Yes."

Hewitt lifted the bolt and opened the door. Four or five steps led parallel with the face of the wall to a sort of path which ran the whole length of the house on this side, and was only separated from a quiet public lane by a low fence and a thin hedge. Almost opposite a small, light gate stood in the fence, firmly padlocked.

"I see," Hewitt remarked, "your house is placed close against one side of the grounds. Is that the side gate which you always keep locked?"

Mrs. Seton replied in the affirmative, and Hewitt laid his hand on the gate in question. "Still," he said, "if security is the object I should recommend hinges a little less rural in pattern; see here," and he gave the gate a jerk upward, lifting the hinge-pins from their sockets and opening the gate from that side, the padlock acting as hinge. "Those hinges," he added, "were meant for a heavier gate than that," and he replaced the gate.

"Yes," Mrs. Seton replied; "I am obliged to you; but that doesn't concern us now. The French window was bolted on the inside. Would you like to see the servants?"

The servants were produced, and Hewitt questioned each in turn, but not one would admit having seen anything of Master Charles Seton after he had been left in the small morning-room. A rather stupid groom fancied he had seen Master Charles on the side lawn, but then remembered that that must have been the day before. The cook, an uncommonly thin, sharp-featured woman for one of her trade, was especially positive that she had not seen him all that day. "And she would be sure to have remembered if she had seen him leaving the house," she said, "because she was the more particular since he was lost the last time."

This was news to Hewitt. "Lost the last time?" he asked; "why, what is this, Mrs. Seton? Was he lost once before?"

"Oh, yes," Mrs. Seton answered, "six or seven weeks ago. But that was quite different. He strayed out at the front gate and was brought back from the police station in the evening."

"But this may be most important," Hewitt said. "You should certainly have told me. Tell me now exactly what happened on this first occasion."

"But it was really quite an ordinary sort of accident. He was left alone and got out through an open gate. Of course we were very anxious; but we had him back the same evening. Need we waste time in talking about that?"

"But it will be no waste of time, I assure you. What was it that happened, exactly?"

"Nurse was about to take him for a short walk just before lunch. On the front lawn he suddenly remembered a whip which had been left in the nursery and insisted on taking it with him. She left him and went back for it, taking however some little time to find it. When she returned he was nowhere to be seen; but one of the gates was a couple of feet or more open—it had caught on a loose stone in swinging to—and no doubt he had wandered off that way. A lady found him some distance away and, not knowing to whom he belonged, took him that evening to a police station, and as messages had been sent to the police stations, we had him back soon after he was left there."

"Do you know who the lady was?"

"Her name was Mrs. Clark. She left her name and address at the police station, and of course I wrote to thank her. But there was some mistake in taking it down, I suppose, for the letter was returned marked not known.'"

"Then you never saw this lady yourself?"

"No."

"I think I will make a note of the exact description of the child and then visit the police station to which this lady took him six weeks ago. Fair, curly hair, I think, and blue eyes? Age two years and three months; walks and runs well, and speaks fairly plainly. Dress?"

"Pale blue llama frock with lace, white under-linen, linen overall, pale blue silk socks and tan shoes. Everything good as new except the shoes, which were badly worn at the backs through a habit he has of kicking back and downward with his heels when sitting. They were rather old shoes, and only used indoors."

"If I remember aright nothing was said of those shoes in the printed bill?"

"Was that so? No, I believe not. I have been so worried."

"Yes, Mrs. Seton, of course. It is most creditable in you to have kept up so well while I have been making my inquiries. Go now and take a good rest while I do what is possible. By the way, where was Mr. Seton yesterday morning when you missed the boy?"

"In the City. He has some important business in hand just now."

"And to-day?"

"He has gone to the City again. Of course he is sadly worried; but he saw that everything possible was done, and his business was very important."

"Just so. Mr. Seton was not married before, I presume—if I may?"

"No, certainly not; why do you ask?"

"I beg your pardon, but I have a habit of asking almost every question I can think of; I can't know too much of a case, you know, and most unlikely pieces of information sometimes turn out useful. Thank you for your patience; I will try another plan now."

Mrs. Seton had kept up remarkably well during Hewitt's examination, but she was plainly by no means a strong woman, and her maid came again to her assistance as Hewitt left. Hewitt himself made for the police station. Few inspectors indeed of the Metropolitan Police force did not know Hewitt by sight, and the one here in charge knew him well. He remembered very well the occasion, six weeks or so before, when Mrs. Clark brought Mrs. Seton's child to the station. He was on duty himself at the time, and he turned up the book containing an entry on the subject. From this it appeared that the lady gave the address' No. 89 Sedgby Road, Belsize Park.

"I suppose you didn't happen to know the lady," Hewitt asked—"by sight or otherwise?"

"No, I didn't, and I'm not sure I could swear to her again," the inspector answered. "She wore a heavy veil, and I didn't see much of her face. One rum thing I noticed though: she seemed rather fond of the baby, and as she stooped down to kiss him before she went away I could see an old scar on her throat. It was just the sort of scar I've seen on a man that's had his throat cut and got over it. She wore a high collar to hide it, but stooping shifted the collar, and so I saw it."

"Did she seem an educated woman?"

"Oh yes; perfect lady; spoke very nice. I told her a baby had been inquired after by Mrs. Seton, and from the description I'd no doubt this was the one. And so it was."

"At what time was this?"

"7.10 p.m. exactly. Here it is, all entered properly."

"Now as to Sedgby Road, Belsize Park. Do you happen to know it?"

"Oh, yes, very well. Very quiet, respectable road indeed. I only know it through walking through."

"I see a suburban directory on the shelf behind you. Do you mind pulling it down? Thanks. Let us find Sedgby Road. Here it is. See, there is no No. 89; the highest number is 67."

"No more there is," the inspector answered, running his finger down the column; "and there's no Clark in the road, that's more. False address, that's plain. And so they've lost him again, have they? We had notice yesterday, of course, and I've just got some bills. This last seems a queer sort of affair, don't it? Child sitting inside the house disappeared like a ghost, and all the doors and windows fastened inside."

Hewitt agreed that the affair had very uncommon features, and presently left the station and sought a cab. All the way back to his office he considered the matter deeply. As a matter of fact he was at a loss. Certain evidence he had seen in the house, but it went a very little way, and beyond that there was merely no clue whatever. There were features of the child's first estrayal also that attracted him, though it might very easily be the case that nothing connected the two events. There was an unknown woman—apparently a lady—who had once had her throat cut, bringing the child back after several hours and giving a false name and address, for since the address was false the same was probably the case with the name. Why was this? This time the child was still absent, and nothing whatever was there to suggest in what direction he might be followed, neither was there anything to indicate why he should be detained anywhere, if detained he was. Hewitt determined, while awaiting any result that the bills might bring, to cause certain inquiries to be made into the antecedents of the Setons. Moreover other work was waiting, and the Seton business must be put aside for a few hours at least.

Hewitt sat late in his office that evening, and at about nine o'clock Mrs. Seton returned. The poor woman seemed on the verge of serious illness. She had received two anonymous letters, which she brought with her, and with scarcely a word placed before Hewitt's eyes.

The first he opened and read as follows:—

"The writer observes that you are offering a reward for the recovery of your child. There is no necessity for this; Charley is quite safe, happy, and in good hands. Pray do not instruct detectives or take any such steps just yet. The child is well and shall be returned to you. This I swear solemnly. His errand is one of mercy; pray have patience."

Hewitt turned the letter and envelope in his hand. "Good paper, of the same sort as the envelope," he remarked, "but only a half sheet, freshly torn off, probably because the other side bore an address heading; therefore most likely from a respectable sort of house. The writing is a woman's, and good, though the writer was agitated when she did it. Posted this afternoon, at Willesden."

"You see," Mrs. Seton said anxiously, "she knows his name. She calls him Charley.'"

"Yes," Hewitt answered; "there may be something in that, or there may not. The name Charles Seton is on the bills, isn't it? And they have been visible publicly all day to-day. So that the name may be more easily explained than some other parts of the letter. For instance, the writer says that the child's errand' is one of mercy. The little fellow may be very intelligent-no doubt is—but children of two years old as a rule do not practise errands of mercy—nor indeed errands of any sort. Can you think of anything whatever, Mrs. Seton, in connection with your family history, or indeed anything else, that may throw light on that phrase?"

He looked keenly at her as he asked, but her expression was one of blank doubt merely, as she shook her head slowly and answered in the negative. Hewitt turned to the other letter and read this:—

"Madam,—If you want your child you had better make an arrangement with Die. You fancy he has strayed, but as a matter of fact he has been stolen, and you little know by whom. You will never get him back except through me, you may rest assured of that. Are you prepared to pay me one hundred pounds (£100) if I hand him to you, and no questions asked? Your present reward, £20, is paltry; and you may finally bid good-bye to your child if you will not accept my terms. If you do, say as much in an advertisement to the Standard, addressed to Veritas."

"A man's handwriting," Hewitt commented; "fairly well formed, but shaky. The writer is not in first-rate health—each line totters away in a downward slope at the end. I shouldn't be surprised to hear that the gentleman drank. Postmark, 'Hampstead'; posted this afternoon also. But the striking thing is the paper and envelope. They are each of exactly the same kind and size as those of the other letter. The paper also is a half sheet, and torn off on the same side as the other; confirmation of my suspicion that the object is to get rid of the printed address. I shall be surprised if both these were not written in the same house. That looks like a traitor in the enemy's camp; the question is winch is the traitor?" Hewitt regarded the letters intently for a few seconds and then proceeded. "Plainly," he said, "if these letters are written by people who know anything about the matter, one writer is lying. The woman promises that the child shall be returned, without reward or search, and talks generally as if the taking away of the child, or the estrayal, or whatever it was, were a very virtuous sort of proceeding. The man says plainly that the child has been stolen, with no attempt to gloss the matter, and asserts that nothing will get the child back but heavy blackmail—a very different story. On the other hand, can there be any concerted design in these two letters? Are they intended, each from its own side, to play up to a certain result?" Hewitt paused and thought. Then he asked suddenly: "Do you recognise anything familiar either in the handwriting or the stationery of these letters?"

"No, nothing."

"Very well," Hewitt said, "we will come to closer quarters with the blackmailer, I think. You needn't commit yourself to paying anything, of course."

"But, Mr. Hewitt, I will gladly pay or do anything. The hundred pounds is nothing. I will pay it gladly if I can only get my child."

"Well, well, we shall see. The man may not be able to do what he offers after all, but that we will test. It is too late now for an advertisement in to-morrow morning's Standard, but there is the Evening Standard—he may even mean that—and the next morning's. I will have an advertisement inserted in both, inviting this man to make an appointment, and prove the genuineness of his offer; that will fetch him if he wants the money, and can do anything for it. Have you nothing else to tell me?"

"Nothing. But have you ascertained nothing yourself? Don't say I've to pass another night in such dreadful suspense."

"I'm afraid, Mrs. Seton, I must ask you to be patient a little longer. I have ascertained something, but it has not carried me far as yet. Remember that if there is anything at all in these anonymous letters (and I think there is) the child is at any rate safe, and to be found one way or another. Both agree in that." This he said mainly to comfort his client, for in fact he had learned very little. His news from the City as to Mr. Seton's early history had been but meagre. He was known as a successful speculator, and that was almost all. There was an indefinite notion that he had been married once before, but nothing more.

All the next day Hewitt did nothing in the case. Another affair, a previous engagement, kept him hard at work in his office all day, and indeed had this not been the case he could have done little. His City inquiries were still in progress, and he awaited, moreover, a reply to the advertisement. But at about half-pest seven in the evening this telegram arrived—

CHILD RETURNED. COME AT ONCE.—SETON.

In five minutes Hewitt was making northwest in a hansom, and in half an hour he was ringing the bell at the Setons' house. Within, Mrs. Seton was still semi-hysterical, clasping the child—an intelligent-looking little fellow—in her arms, and refusing to release her hold of him for a moment. Mr. Seton stood before the fire in the same room. He was a smart-looking, scrupulously dressed man of thirty-five or thereabouts, and he began explaining his telegram as soon as he had wished Hewitt good evening.

"The child's back," he said, "and of course that's the great thing. But I'm not satisfied, Mr. Hewitt. I want to know why it was taken away, and I want to punish somebody. It's really very extraordinary. My poor wife has been driving about all day—she called on you, by the bye, but you were out," (Hewitt credited this to Kerrett, who had been told he must not be disturbed) "and she has been all over the place uselessly, unable to rest, of course. Well, I have been at home since half-past four, and at about six I was smoking in the small morning-room—I often use it as a smoking-room—and looking out at the French window. I came away from there, and half an hour or more later, as it was getting dusk, I remembered I had left the French window open, and sent a servant to shut it. She went straight to the room, and there on the floor, where he was seen last, she found the child playing with his toys as though nothing had happened!"

"And how was he dressed—as he is now?"

"Yes, just as he was when we missed him."

Hewitt stepped up to the child as he sat on his mother's lap, and rubbed his cheek, speaking pleasantly to him. The little fellow looked up and smiled, and Hewitt observed: "One thing is noticeable: this linen overall is almost clean. Little boys like this don't keep one white overall clean for three days, do they? And see—those shoes—aren't they new? Those he had were old, I think you said, and tan coloured."

The shoes now on the child's feet were of white leather, with a noticeable sewn ornamentation in silk. His mother had not noticed them before, and as she looked he lifted his little foot higher and said. "Look, mummy, more new shoes!"

"Ask him," suggested Hewitt hurriedly, "who gave them to him."

His father asked him and the little fellow looked puzzled. After a pause he said "Mummy."

"No," his mother answered, "I didn't."

He thought a moment and then said, "No, no, not his mummy—course not." And for some little while after that the only answer procurable from him was "Course not," which seemed to be a favourite phrase of his.

"Have you asked him where he has been?"

"Yes," his mother answered, "but he only says 'Ta-ta.'"

"Ask him again."

She did. This time, after a little reflection, he pointed his chubby arm toward the door and said. "Been dere."

"Who took you?" asked Mrs. Seton.

Again Charley seemed puzzled. Then, looking doubtfully at his mother, he said "Mummy."

"No, not mummy," she answered, and his reply was "Course not," after which he attempted to climb on her shoulder.

Then, at Hewitt's suggestion, he was asked whom he went to see. This time the reply was prompt.

"Poor daddy," he said.

"What, this daddy?"

"No, not vis daddy—course not." And that was all that could be got from him.

"He will probably say things in the next day or two which may be useful," Hewitt said, "if you listen pretty sharply. Now I should like to go to the small morning-room."

In time room in question the door was still open. Outside the moon had risen and made the evening almost as clear as day. Hewitt examined the steps and the path at their foot, but all was dry and hard and showed no footmark. Then, as his eye rested on the small gate, "See here," he exclaimed suddenly; "somebody has been in, lifting the gate as I showed Mrs. Seton when I was last here. The gate has been replaced in a hurry and only the top hinge has dropped in its place; the bottom one is disjointed." He lifted time gate once more and set it back. The ground just along its foot was softer than in the parts surrounding, and here Hewitt perceived the print of a heel. It was the heel-mark of a woman's boot, small and sharp and of the usual curved D -shape. Nowhere else within or without was there the slightest mark. Hewitt went some distance either way in the outer lane, but without discovering anything more.

"I think I will borrow those new shoes," Hewitt said on his return. "I think I should be disposed to investigate further in any case, for my own satisfaction. The thing interests me. By the way, Mrs. Seton, tell me, would these shoes be more likely to have been bought at a regular shoemaker's or at a baby-linen shop?"

"Certainly, I should say at a baby-linen shop," Mrs. Seton answered; "they are of excellent quality, and for babies' shoes of this fancy description one would never go to an ordinary shoemaker's."

"So much the better, because the baby-linen shops are fewer than the shoemakers'. I may take these, then? Perhaps before I go you had better make quite certain that there is nothing else not your own about the child."

There was nothing, and with the shoes in his pocket Hewitt regained his cab and travelled back to his office. The case, from its very bareness and simplicity, puzzled him. Why was the child taken? Plainly not to keep, for it had been returned almost as it went. Plainly also not for the sake of reward or blackmail, for here was the child safely back, before the anonymous blackmailer had had a chance of earning his money. More, the advertised reward had not been claimed. Also it could not be a matter of malice or revenge, for the child was quite unharmed, and indeed seems to have been quite happy. No conceivable family complication previous to the marriage of Mr. and Mrs. Seton could induce anybody to take away and return the child, which was undoubtedly Mrs. Seton's. Then who could be the "poor daddy" and "mummy"—not "vis daddy" and not "vis mummy "—that the child had been with. The Setons knew nothing of them. It was difficult to see what it could all mean.

Arrived at his office Hewitt took a map, and, setting the leg of a pair of compasses on the site of the Setons' house, described a circle, including in its radius all Willesden and Hampstead. Then, with the Suburban Directory to help him, he began searching out and noting all the baby-linen shops in the area. After all, there were not many—about a dozen. This done, Hewitt went home.

In the morning he began his hunt. His design was to call at each of the shops until he laid found in which a pair of shoes of that particular pattern had been sold on the day of little Charley Seton's disappearance. The first two shops he tried did not keep shoes of the pattern, and had never had them, and the young ladies behind the counter seemed vastly amused at Hewitt's inquiries. Nothing perturbed, he tried the next shop on his list in the Hampstead district. There they kept such shoes as a rule, but were "out of them at present." Hewitt immediately sent his card to the proprietress requesting a few minutes' interview. The lady—a very dignified lady indeed—in black silk, gray corkscrew curls and spectacles, came out with Hewitt's card between her fingers. He apologised for troubling her, and, stepping out of hearing from the counter, explained that his business was urgent.

"A child has been taken away by some unauthorised person, whom I am endeavouring to trace. This person bought this pair of shoes on Monday. You keep such shoes, I find, though they are not in stock at present, and, as they appear to be of an uncommon sort, possibly they were bought here."

The lady looked at them. "Yes," she said, "this pattern of shoe is made especially for me. I do not think you can buy them at other places."

"Then may I ask you to inquire from your assistants if any were sold on Monday, and to whom?"

"Certainly." Then there were consultations behind counters and desks, and examinations of carbon-papered books. In the end the proprietress came to Hewitt, followed by a young lady of rather pert and self-confident aspect. "We find," she said, "that two pairs of these shoes were sold on Monday. But one pair was afterwards brought back and exchanged for others less expensive. This young lady sold both."

"Ah, then possibly she may remember something of the person who bought the pair which was not exchanged."

"Yes," the assistant answered at once, addressing herself to the lady, "it was Mrs. Butcher's servant."

The proprietress frowned slightly. "Oh, indeed," she said, "Mrs. Butcher's servant, was it. There have been inquiries about Mrs. Butcher before, I believe, though not here. Mrs. Butcher is a woman who takes babies to mind, and is said to make a trade of adopting them, or finding people anxious to adopt them. I know nothing of her, nor do I want to. She lives somewhere not far off, and you can get her address, I believe, from the greengrocer's round the corner."

"Does she keep more than one servant?"

"Oh, I think not; but no doubt the greengrocer can say." The lady seemed to feel it an affront that she should be supposed to know anything of Mrs. Butcher, and Hewitt consequently started for the greengrocer's. Now this was just one of those cases in which dependence on information given by other people put Hewitt on the wrong scent. He spent that day in a fatiguing pursuit of Mrs. Butcher's servant, with adventures rather amusing in themselves, but quite irrelevant to the Seton case. In the end, when he had captured her, and proceeded to open a cunning battery of inquiries, under plea of a bet with a friend that the shoes could not be matched, he soon found that she had been the purchaser who, after buying just such a pair of shoes, had returned and exchanged them for something cheaper. And the only outcome of his visit to the baby-linen shop was the waste of a day. It was indeed just one of those checks which, while they may hamper the progress of a narrative for popular reading, are nevertheless inseparable from the matter-of-fact experience of Hewitt's profession.

With a very natural rage in his heart, but with as polite an exterior as possible, Hewitt returned to the baby-linen shop in the evening. The whole case seemed barren of useful evidence, and at each turn as yet he had found himself helpless. At the shop the self-confident young lady calmly admitted that soon after he had left something had caused her to remember that it was the other customer who had kept the white shoes and not Mrs. Butcher's servant.

"And do you know the other customer?" he asked.

"No, she was quite a stranger. She brought in a little boy from a cab and bought a lot of things for him—a suit of outdoor clothes, as well as the shoes."

"Ah! now probably this is what I want. Can you remember anything of the child?"

"Yes, he was a pretty little fellow, about two years old or so, with curls. She called him Charley."

"Did she put the things on him in the shop?"

"Not the frock; but she put on the outer coat, the hat and the shoes. I can remember it all now quite well, now I have had time to think."

"Then what shoes did the child wear when he came in?"

"Rather old tan-coloured ones."

"Then I think this is the person I am after. You say you never saw her at any other time before or since. Try to describe her."

"Well, she was a lady well dressed, in black. She had a very high collar to hide a scar on her neck, like the scars people have sometimes after abscesses, I think. I could see it from the side when she stooped down."

"And are you sure she had nothing sent home? Did she take everything with her?"

"Yes; nothing was sent, else we should know her address, you know."

"She didn't happen to pay with a banknote, did she?"

"No, in cash."

Hewitt left with little more ceremony and made the best of his way to his friend the inspector at the police station. Here was the woman with the scarred neck again—Charley's deliverer once, now his kidnapper. If only something else could be ascertained of her—some small clue that might bring her identity into view—the thing would be done.

At the station, however, there was something new. A man had just come in, very drunk, and had given himself into custody for kidnapping the child Charles Seton, whose description was set forth on the bill which still appeared on the notice-hoard outside the station. When Hewitt arrived the man was lolling, wretched and maudlin, against the rail, and, oblivious of most of the questions addressed to him, was ranting and snivelling by turns. His dress was good, though splashed with mud, and his bloated face, bleared eyes and loose, tremulous mouth proclaimed the habitual drunkard.

"I shay I'll gimmeself up," he proclaimed, with a desperate attempt at dignity; "I'll gimmeself up takin' away lil boy; I'll shacrifishe m'self. Solemn duty shacrifishe m'self f'elpless woman, ain't it? Ver' well then; gimmeself up takin' 'way lil boy, buyin' 'm pair shoes. No harm in that, issher? Hope not. Ver' well then." And be subsided into tears.

"What's your name?" asked the inspector.

"Whash name? Thash my bishnesh. Warrer wan' know name for? Grapert—hence ask gellum'sh name. I'm gellum, thash whit' I am. Besht of shisters too, besht shis'ers"—snivelling again—"an' I'm ungra'ful beasht. But I shacrifishe 'self; she shun' get 'n trouble. D'year? Gimmeself up shtealin' lil boy. Who says I ain' gellum?"

Nothing more intelligible than this could be got out of him, and presently he was taken off to the cells. Then Hewitt asked the inspector, "What will happen to him now?"

The inspector laughed.

"Oh he'll get very sober and sick and sorry by the morning," he said; "and then he'll have to send home for some money, that's all."

"And as to the child?"

"Oh, he'll forget all about that; that's only a drunken freak. The child has been recovered. You know that, I suppose?"

"Yes, but I am still after the person who took it away. It was a woman. Indeed I've more than a suspicion that it was the woman who brought the child here when he was lost before—the one with the scar on the neck, you know."

"Is that so?" said the inspector. "Well, that's a rum go, ain't it? What did she bring him back here for if she wanted him again?"

"That I want to find out," Hewitt answered. "And now I want you to do me a favour. You say you expect that man below will want to send home in the morning for money. Well, I want to be the messenger."

The inspector opened his eyes.

"Want to be the messenger? Well, that's easily done; if you're here at the time I'll leave word. But why?"

"Well, I've a sort of notion I know something about his family, and I want to make sure. Shall I be here at eight in the morning, or shall we say nine?"

"Which you like; I expect he'll be shouting for bail before eight."

"Very well, we will say eight. Goodnight."

And so Hewitt had to let yet another night go without an explanation of the mystery; but he felt that his hand was on the key at last, though it had only fallen there by chance. Prompt to his time at eight in the morning he was at the police-station, where another inspector was now on duty, who, however, had been told of Hewitt's wish.

"Ah," he said, "you're well to time, Mr. Hewitt. That prisoner's as limp as rags now; he's begging of us to send to his sister."

"Does he say anything about that child?"

"Says he don't know anything about it; all a drunken freak. His name's Oliver Neale, and he lives at 10 Morton Terrace, Hampstead, with his sister. Her name's Mrs. Isitt, and you're to take this note and bring her back with you, or at any rate some money; and you're to say he's truly repentant," the inspector concluded with a grin.

The distance was short, and Hewitt walked it. Morton Terrace was a short row of pleasant old-fashioned villas, ivy-grown and neat, and No. 10 was as neat as any. To the servant who answered his ring Hewitt announced himself as a gentleman with a message from Mrs. Isitt's brother. This did not seem to prepossess the girl in Hewitt's favour, and she backed to the end of the hall and communicated with somebody on the stairs before finally showing Hewitt into a room, where he was quickly followed by Mrs. Isitt.

She was a rather tall woman of perhaps thirty-eight, and had probably been attractive, though now her face bore lines of sad grief. Hewitt noticed that she wore a very high black collar.

"Good-morning, Mrs. Isitt," he said. "I'm afraid my errand is not altogether pleasant. The fact is your brother, Mr. Neale, was not altogether sober last night, and he is now at the police station, where he wrote this note."

Mrs. Isitt did not appear surprised, and took the note with no more than a sigh.

"Yes," she said, "it can't be concealed. This is not the first time by many, as you probably know, if you are a friend of his."

She read the note, and as she looked up Hewitt said—

"No, I have not known him long. I happened to be at the station last night, and he rather attracted my attention by insisting, in his intoxicated state, on giving himself up for kidnapping a child, Charles Seton."

Mrs. Isitt started as though shot. Pale of cheek, she glanced fearfully in Hewitt's face and there met a keen gaze that seemed to read her brain. She saw that her secret was known, but for a moment she struggled, and her lips worked convulsively—

"Charles Seton—Charles Seton?" she said.

"Yes, Mrs. Isitt, that is the name. The child, as a matter of fact, was stolen by the person who bought these shoes for it. Do you recognise them?"

He produced the shoes and held them before her. The woman sank on the sofa behind her, terrified, but unable to take her eyes from Hewitt's.

"Come, Mrs. Isitt," he said, "you have been recognised. Here is my card. I am commissioned by the parents of the child to find who removed him, and I think I have succeeded."

She took the card and glanced at it dazedly; then she sank with a groaning sob with her face on the head of the sofa, and as she did so Hewitt could see a scar on the side of her neck peeping above her high collar.

"Oh, my God!" the woman moaned. "Then it has come to this. He will die! he will die!"

The woman's anguish was piteous to see. Hewitt had gained his point, and was willing to spare her. He placed his hand on her heaving shoulder and begged her not to distress herself.

"The matter is rather difficult to understand, Mrs. Isitt," he said. "If you will compose yourself perhaps you can explain. I can assure you that there is no desire to be vindictive. I'm afraid my manner upset you. Pray reassure yourself. May I sit down?"

Nobody could by his manner more easily restore confidence and trust than Hewitt, when it pleased him. Mrs. Isitt lifted her head and gazed at him once more with a troubled though quieter expression.

"I think you wrote Mrs. Seton an anonymous letter," Hewitt said, producing the first of those which Mrs. Seton had brought him. "It was kind of you to reassure the poor woman."

"Oh, tell me," Mrs. Isitt asked, "was she much upset at missing the little boy? Did it make her ill?"

"She was upset, of course; but perhaps the joy of recovering him compensated for all."

"Yes; I took him back as soon as I possibly could, really I did, Mr. Hewitt. And, oh! I was so tempted! My life has been so unhappy! If you only knew!" She buried her face in her hands.

"Will you tell me?" Hewitt suggested gently. "You see, whatever happens, an explanation of some sort is the first thing."

"Yes, yes—of course. Oh, I am a wretched woman." She paused for some little while, and then went on: "Mr. Hewitt, my husband is a lunatic." She paused again.

"There was never a man, Mr. Hewitt, so devoted to his wife and children as my husband. He bore even with the continual annoyance of my brother, whom you saw, because he was my brother. But a little more than a year ago, as the result of an accident, a tumour formed on his brain. The thing is incurable except, as a remote possibility, by a most dangerous operation, which the doctors fear to attempt except under most favourable conditions. Without that he must die sooner or later. Meantime he is insane, though with many and sometimes long intervals of perfect lucidity. When the disease attacked him there was little warning, except from pains in the head, till one dreadful night. Then he rose from bed a maniac and killed our child, a little girl of six, whom he was devotedly attached to. He also cut my own throat with his razor, but I recovered. I would rather say nothing more of that—it is too dreadful, though indeed I think about little else. There was another child, a baby boy, about a year old when his sister died, and he—he died of scarlet fever scarcely four months ago.

"My husband was taken to a private asylum at Willesden, where he now is. I visited him frequently, and took the baby, and it was almost terrible to see—a part of his insanity, no doubt—how his fondness for that child grew. When it died I never dared to tell him. Indeed the doctors forbade it. In his state he would have died raving. But he asked for it, sometimes earnestly, sometimes angrily, till I almost feared to visit him. Then he began to demand it of the doctors and attendants, and his excitement increased day by day. I was told to prepare for the worst. When I visited him he sometimes failed to recognise me, and at others demanded the child fiercely. I should tell you that it was only just about this time that it was found that the tumour existed, and the idea of the operation was suggested; but of course it was impossible in his disturbed condition. I scarcely dared to go to see him, and yet I did so long to! Dr. Bailey did indeed suggest that possibly we might find he would be quieted by being shown another child; but I myself felt that to be very unlikely.

"It was while things were in this state, and about six or seven weeks ago, that, walking toward Cricklewood one morning, I saw a little fellow trotting along all alone, who actually startled me—startled me very much—by his resemblance to our poor little one. The likeness was one of those extraordinary ones that one only finds among young children. This child was a little bigger and stronger than ours was when he died, but then it was older—probably very nearly the age and size our own would have been had it lived. Nobody else was in sight, and I fancied the child looked about to cry, so I went to it and spoke. Plainly it had strayed, and could not tell me where it lived, only that its name was Charley. I took it in my arms and it grew quite friendly. As I talked to it suddenly Dr. Bailey's suggestion came in my mind. If any child could deceive my poor husband surely this was the one. Of course I should have to find its parents—probably through the police; but why not at any rate take it to Willesden in the meantime for an hour or so? I could not resist the temptation—I took the first available cab.

"The result of the experiment almost frightened me. My poor husband received the child with transports of delight, kissed it, and laughed and wept over it like a mother rather than a father, and refused to give it up for hours. The child of course would not answer to its strange name at first, but he seemed an adaptable little thing, and presently began calling my poor husband 'daddy.' I had not been so happy myself for months as I was as I watched them. I. had told Dr. Bailey—what I fear was not strictly true—that I had borrowed the child from a friend. At length I felt I must go and take the boy to the police, and with great difficulty I managed to get it away, my poor husband crying like a child. Well, I took the little fellow to the station I judged nearest to where I found him, and gave him up to the care of the inspector. But I was a little frightened at having kept him so long, and gave a false name and address. Still I learned from the inspector that the child had been inquired after, and by whom.

"My husband was quiet for some days after this, but then he began to ask for his boy with more vehemence than ever. He grew worse and worse, and soon his ravings were terrible. Dr. Bailey urged me to bring the child again, but what could I do? I formed a desperate idea of going to Mrs. Seton, telling her the whole thing, and imploring her to let me take the child again. But then would that be likely? Would she allow her child to be placed in the arms of a lunatic—one indeed who had already killed a child of his own? I felt that the thing was impossible. Still I went to the house and walked about it again and again, I scarcely knew why. And my poor husband in his confinement screamed for his child till I dared not go near him. So it was when one morning—last Monday morning—I had passed the front of the Setons' house and turned up the lane at the side. I could see over the low fence and hedge, and as I came to the French window with the steps I saw that the window was open at one side and little Charley was standing on the top step. He recognised me, smiled and called just as my own child would have done; indeed as I stood there I almost fell into the delusion of my poor mad husband. I took the gate in my hands, shaking it impatiently, and in attempting to open it from the wrong end, found the hinges lift out. I could see that nobody else was in the room behind the French window. There was the temptation—the overwhelming temptation—and I was distracted. I took the little fellow hurriedly in my anus and pulled the window to, so that the bottom bolt fell into the floor socket; then I replaced the gate as I found it and ran to where I knew there was a cabstand. Oh! Mr. Hewitt, was it so very sinful? And I meant to bring him back that same afternoon, I really did.

"The child was in indoor clothes, and had no hat. I called at a baby-linen shop and bought hat, cloak, frock and a new pair of shoes. Then I hurried to Willesden. Again the effect was magical. My husband was happy once more; but when at last I attempted to take the child away he would not let it go. It was terrible. Oh, I can't describe the scene. Dr. Bailey told me that, come what might, I must stay that night in a room his wife would provide for me and keep the child, or perhaps I must sit up with my husband and let the child sleep on my knee. In the end it was the latter that I did.

"By the morning my senses were blunted and I scarcely cared what happened. I determined that as I had gone so far I would keep the child that day at least; indeed, as I say, whether by the influence of my husband I know not, but I almost felt myself falling into his delusion that the child was ours. I went home for an hour at midday, taking the child, and then my wretched brother saw it and got the whole story from me. He told me that reward bills were out about the child, and then I dimly realised that its mother must be suffering pain, and I wrote the note you spoke of. Perhaps I had some little idea of delaying pursuit—I don't know. At any rate I wrote it, and posted it at Willesden as I went back. My husband had been asleep when I left, but now he was awake again and asking for the child once more. There is little more to say. I stayed that night and the next day, and by that time my husband had become tranquil and rational as he had not been for months. If only the improvement can be sustained they think of operating to-morrow or the next day.

"I carried Charley back in the dusk, intending to put him inside one of the gates, ring, and watch him safely in from a little way off, but as I passel down the side lane I saw the French window open again and nobody near. I had been that way before and felt bolder there. I took his hat and cloak (I had already changed his frock) and, after kissing him, put him hastily through the window and came away. But I had forgotten the new shoes. I remembered them, however, when I got home, and immediately conceived a fear that the child's parents might trace me by their means. I mentioned this fear to my brother, and it appeared to frighten him. He borrowed some money of me yesterday, and it seems got intoxicated. In that state he is always anxious to do some noble action, through he is capable, I am grieved to say, of almost any meanness when sober. He lives here at my expense, indeed, and borrows money from his friends for drink. These may seem hard things for a sister to say, but everybody knows it. He has wearied me, and I have lost all shame of him. I suppose in his muddled state he got the notion that he would accuse himself of what I had done and so shield me. I expect he repented of his self-sacrifice this morning though."

Hewitt knew that he had, but said nothing. Also he said nothing of the anonymous letter he had in his pocket, wherein Mr. Oliver Neale had covertly demanded a hundred pounds for the restoration of Charley Seton. Ho guessed however that that gentleman had feared making the appointment that the advertisement answering his letter had suggested.

To Mr. and Mrs. Seton Hewitt told the whole story, omitting at first names and addresses. "I saw plainly," he said in course of his talk, "that the child might easily have been taken from the French window. I did not say so, for Mrs. Seton was already sufficiently distressed, and the notion that the child was kidnapped and not simply lost might have made her worse just then. The toys—the cart with the string on it in particular—had been dragged in the direction of the window, and then nothing would be easier than for the child to open the window itself. There was nothing but a drop bolt, working very easily, which the child must often have seen lifted, and you will remember that the catch did not act. Once the child had opened the window and got outside, the whole thing was simple. The gate could be lifted, the child taken, and the window pulled to, so that the bolt would fall into its place and leave all as before.

"As to the previous occasion, I thought it curious at first that the child should stray before lunch and yet not be heard of again till the evening, and then apparently not be over-fatigued. But beyond these little things, and what I inferred from the letter, I had very little to help me indeed. Nothing, in fact, till I got the shoes, and they didn't carry me very far. The drunken rant of the man in the police station attracted me because he spoke not only of taking away the child, but of buying it Shoes. Now nobody could know of the buying of the shoes who did not know something more. But I knew it was a woman who had taken Charley, as you know, from the heel-mark and the evidence of the shop people, so that when the bemused fool talked of his sister, and sacrificing himself for her, and keeping her out of trouble, and so on, I arranged the case up in my mind, and, so far as I ventured, I guessed it aright. The police inspector knew nothing of the matter of the shoes, nor of the fact of the person I was after being a woman, so thought the thing no more-than a drunken freak.

"And now," Hewitt said, "before I tell you this woman's name, don't you think the poor creature has suffered enough?"

Both Mrs. Seton and her husband agreed that she had, and that so far as they were concerned no further steps should be taken. And when she was told where to go, Mrs. Seton went off at once to offer Mrs. Isitt her forgiveness and sympathy. But Mrs. Isitt's punishment came in twenty-four hours, when her husband died in the surgeon's hands.

II. — THE CASE OF MR. GELDARD'S ELOPEMENT

I

Any people have been surprised at the information that, in all Martin Hewitt's wide and busy practice, the matrimonial cases whereon he has been engaged have been comparatively few. That he has had many important cases of the sort is true, but among the innumerable cases of different descriptions they make a small percentage. The reason is that so many of the persons wishing to consult him on such concerns were actuated by mere unreasoning or fanciful jealousy that Hewitt would do no more in their cases than urge reconciliation and mutual trust, The common "private inquiry" offices chiefly flourish on this class of case, and their proprietors present no particular reluctance to taking it up. In any event it means fees for consultation and "watching;" and recent newspaper reports have made it plain that among some of the less scrupulous agents a case may be manufactured from beginning to end according to order. Again, Hewitt had a distaste for the sort of work commonly involved in matrimonial troubles; and with the immense amount of business brought to him, rendering necessary his rejection of so many commissions, it was easy for him to avoid what went against his inclinations. Still, as I have said, matrimonial cases there were, and often of an interesting nature, taking rise in no fanciful nor unreasoning jealousy.

When, on its change of proprietorship, I accepted my appointment on the paper that now claims me, I had a week or two's holiday pending the final turning over of the property. I could not leave town, for I might have been wanted at any moment, but I made an absorbing and instructive use of my leisure as an amateur assistant to Hewitt. I sat in his office much of the time and saw more of the daily routine of his work than I had ever done before; and I was present at one or two interviews that initiated cases that afterwards developed striking features. One of these—which indeed I saw entirely through before I resumed my more legitimate work—was the case of Mr. and Mrs. Geldard.

Hewitt had stepped out for a few minutes, and I was sitting alone in his private room when I became conscious of some disturbance in the outer office. An excited female voice was audible making impatient inquiries. Presently Kerrett, Hewitt's clerk, came in with the message that a lady—Mrs. Geldard, was the name on the visitor's slip that she had filled up—was anxious to see Mr. Hewitt, at once, and failing himself had decided to see me, whom Kerrett had calmly taken it upon himself to describe as Hewitt's confidential assistant. He apologised for this, and explained that he thought, as the lady seemed excited, it would be as well to let her see me to begin with, if there was no objection, and perhaps she would begin to be coherent and intelligible by Hewitt's arrival, which might occur at any moment. So the lady was shown in. She was tall, bony, and severe of face, and she began as soon as she saw me: "I've come to get you to get a watch set on my husband. I've endured this sort of thing in silence long enough. I won't have it. I'll see if there's no protection to be had for a woman treated as I am—with his goings out all day 'on business' when his office is shut up tight all the time. I wanted to see Mr. Hewitt himself, but I suppose you'll do, for the present at any rate, though I'll have it sifted to the bottom, and get the best advice to be had, no matter what it costs, though I am only a woman with nobody to confide in or to speak a word for me, and I'm not going to be crushed like a fly, as I'll soon let him know."

Here I seized a short opportunity to offer Mrs. Geldard a chair, and to say that I expected Mr. Hewitt in a few minutes.

"Very well, I'll wait and see him. But you have to do with the watching business no doubt, and you'll understand what it is I want done; and I'm sure I'm justified, and mean to sift it to the bottom, whatever happens. Am I to be kept in total ignorance of what my husband does all day when he is supposed to be at business? Is it likely I should submit to that?"

I said I didn't think it likely at all, which was a fact. Mrs. Geldard appeared to be about the least submissive woman I ever saw.

"No, and I won't, that's more. Nice goings on somewhere, no doubt, with his office shut up all day and the business going to ruin. I want you to watch him. I want you to follow him to-morrow morning and find out all he does and let me know. I've followed him myself this morning and yesterday morning, but he gets away somehow from the back of his office, and I can't watch on two staircases at once, so I want you to come and do it, and I'll—"

Here fortunately Hewitt's arrival checked Mrs. Geldard's flow of speech, and I rose and introduced him. I told him shortly that the lady desired a watch to be set on her husband at his office, and a report to be given her of his daily proceedings. Hewitt did not appear to accept the commission with any particular delight, but he sat down to hear his visitor's story. "Stay here, Brett," he said, as he saw my hands stretched towards the door. "We've an engagement presently, you know."

The engagement, I remembered, was merely to lunch, and Hewitt kept me with some notion of restricting the time which this alarming woman might be disposed to occupy. She repeated to Hewitt, in the same manner, what she had already said to me, and then Hewitt, seizing his first opportunity, said, "Will you please tell me, Mrs. Geldard, definitely and concisely, what evidence, or even indication, you have of unbecoming conduct on your husband's part, and substantially what case you wish me to take up?"

"Case? why, I've been telling you." And again Mrs. Geldard repeated her vague catalogue of sufferings, assuring Hewitt that she was determined to have the best advice and assistance, and that therefore she had come to him. In the end Hewitt answered: "Put concisely, Mrs. Geldard, I take it that your case is simply this. Mr. Geldard is in business as, I think you told me, a general agent and broker, and keeps an office in the city. You have had various disagreements with him—not an uncommon thing, unfortunately, between married people—and you have entertained certain indefinite suspicions of his behaviour. Yesterday you went so far as to go to his office soon after he should have been there, and found him absent and the office shut up. You waited some time, and called again, but the door was still locked, and the caretaker of the building assured you that Mr. Geldard usually kept his office thus shut. You knocked repeatedly, and called through the keyhole, but got no answer. This morning you even followed your husband and saw him enter his office, but when, a little later, you yourself attempted to enter it you once more found it locked and apparently tenantless. From this you conclude that he must have left his rooms by some back way, and you say you are determined to find out where he goes and what he does during the day. For this purpose you, I gather, wish me to watch him and report his whole day's proceedings to you?"

"Yes, of course; as I said."

"I'm afraid the state of my other engagements just at present will scarcely admit of that. Indeed, to speak quite frankly, this mere watching, especially of husband or wife, is not a sort of business that I care to undertake, except as a necessary part of some definite, tangible case. But apart from that, will you allow me to advise you? Not professionally, I mean, but merely as a man of the world. Why come to third parties with these vague suspicions? Family divisions of this sort, with all sorts of covert mistrust and suspicion, are bad things at best, and once carried as far as you talk of carrying this, go beyond peaceable remedy. Why not deal frankly and openly with your husband? Why not ask him plainly what he has been doing during the days you were unable to get into his office? You will probably find it all capable of a very simple and innocent explanation."

"Am I to understand, then," Mrs. Geldard said, bridling, "that you refuse to help me?"

"I have not refused to help you," Hewitt replied. "On the contrary, I am trying to help you now. Did your husband ever follow any other profession than the one he is now engaged in?"

"Once he was a mechanical engineer, but he got very few clients, and it didn't pay."

"There, now, is a suggestion. Would it be very unlikely that your husband, trained mechanician as he is, may have reverted so far to his old profession as to be conceiving some new invention? And in that case, what more probable than that he would lock himself securely in his office to work out his idea, and take no notice of visitors knocking, in order to admit nobody who might learn something of what he was doing? Does he keep a clerk or office boy?"

"No, he never has since he left the mechanical engineering."

"Well, Mrs. Geldard, I'm sorry I have no more time now, but I must earnestly repeat my advice. Come to an understanding with your husband in a straightforward way as soon as you possibly can. There are plenty of private inquiry offices about where they will watch anybody, and do almost anything, without any inquiry into their clients' motives, and with a single eye to fees. I charge you no fee, and advise you to treat your husband with frankness."

Mrs. Geldard did not seem particularly satisfied, though Hewitt's rejection of a consultation fee somewhat softened her. She left protesting that Hewitt didn't know the sort of man she had to deal with, and that, one way or another, she must have an explanation.

"Come, we'll get to lunch," said Hewitt. "I'm afraid my suggestion as to Mr. Geldard's probable occupation in his office wasn't very brilliant, but it was the pleasantest I could think of for the moment, and the main thing was to pacify the lady. One does no good by aggravating a misunderstanding of that sort."

"Can you make any conjecture," I said, "at what the trouble really is?"

Hewitt raised his eyebrows and shook his head. "There's no telling," he said: "An angry, jealous, pragmatical woman, apparently, this Mrs. Geldard, and it's impossible to judge at first sight how much she really knows and how much she imagines. I don't suppose she'll take my advice. She seems to have worked herself into a state of rancour that must burst out violently somewhere. But lunch is the present business. Come."

The next day I spent at a friend's house a little way out of town, so that it was not till the following morning, about the same Hewitt that I learned from Hewitt that Mrs. Geldard had called again.

"Yes," he said; "she seems to have taken my advice in her own way, which wasn't a judicious one. When I suggested that she should speak frankly to her husband I meant her to do it in a reasonably amicable mood. Instead of that, she appears to have flown at his throat, so to speak, with all the bitterness at her tongue's disposal. The natural result was a row. The man slanged back, the woman threatened divorce, and the man threatened to leave the country altogether. And so yesterday Mrs. Geldard was here again to get me to follow and watch him. I had to decline once more, and got something rather like a slanging myself for my pains. She seemed to think I was in league with her husband in some way. In the end I promised—more to get rid of her than anything else—to take the case in hand if ever there were anything really tangible to go upon; if her husband really did desert her, you know, or anything like that. If, in fact, there were anything more for me to consider than these spiteful suspicions."

"I suppose," I said, "she had nothing more to tell you than she had before?"

"Very little. She seems to have startled Geldard, however, by a chance shot. It seems that she once employed a maid, whom she subsequently dismissed, because, as she tells me, the young woman was a great deal too good-looking, and because she observed, or fancied she observed, signs of some secret understanding between her maid and her husband.

Moreover, it was her husband who discovered this maid and introduced her into the house, and furthermore, he did all he could to induce Mrs. Geldard not to dismiss her. He even hinted that her dismissal might cause serious trouble, and Mrs. Geldard says it is chiefly since this maid has left the house that his movements have become so mysterious. Well it seems that in the heat of yesterday's quarrel Mrs. Geldard, quite at random, asked tauntingly how many letters Geldard had received from Emma Trennatt lately. Emma Trennatt was the girl's name. This chance shot seemed to hit the target. Geldard (so his wife tells me at any rate) winced visibly, paled a little, and dodged the question. But for the rest of the quarrel he appeared much less at ease, and made more than one attempt to find out how much his wife really knew of the correspondence she had spoken of. But as her reference to it was of course the wildest possible fluke, he got little guidance, while his better-half waxed savage in her triumph, and they parted on wild cat terms. She came straight here and evidently thought that after Geldard's reception of her allusion to correspondence with Emma Trennatt—which she seemed to regard as final and conclusive confirmation of all her jealousies—I should take the case in hand at once. When she found me still disinclined she gave me a trifling sample of her rhetoric, as no doubt commonly supplied to Mr. Geldard. She said in effect that she had only come to me because she meant having the best assistance possible, but that she didn't think much of me after all, and one man was as bad as another, and so on. I think she was a trifle angrier because I remained calm and civil. And she went away this time without the least reference to a consultation fee one way or another."

I laughed. "Probably," I said, "she went off to some agent who'll watch as long as she likes to pay."

"Quite possibly." But we were quite wrong. Hewitt took his hat and we made for the staircase. As we opened the landing-door there were hurried feet on the stairs below, and as it shut behind Mrs. Geldard's bonnet-load of pink flowers hove up before us. She was in a state of fierce alarm and excitement that had oddly enough something of triumph in it, as of the woman who says, "I told you so." Hewitt gave a tragic groan under his breath.

"Here's a nice state of things I'm in for now, Mr. Hewitt," she began abruptly, "through your refusing to do anything for me while there was time, though I was ready to pay you well as I told your young man but no you wouldn't listen to anything and seemed to think you knew my business better than I could tell you and now you've caused this state of affairs by delay perhaps you'll take the case in hand now?"

"But you haven't told me what has happened—" Hewitt began, whereat the lady instantly rejoined, with a shrill pretence of a laugh, "Happened? Why what do you suppose has happened after what I have told you over and over again? My precious husband's gone clean away, that's all. He's deserted me and gone nobody knows where. That's what's happened. You said that if he did anything of that sort you'd take the case up; so now I've come to see if you'll keep your promise. Not that it's likely to be of much use now."

We turned back into Hewitt's private office and Mrs. Geldard told her story. Disentangled from irrelevances, repetitions, opinions and incidental observations, it was this. After the quarrel Geldard had gone to business as usual and had not been seen nor heard of since. After her yesterday's interview with Hewitt Mrs. Geldard had called at her husband's office and found it shut as before. She went home again and waited, but he never returned home that evening, nor all night. In the morning she had gone to the office once more, and finding it still shut had told the caretaker that her husband was missing and insisted on his bringing his own key and opening it for her inspection. Nobody was there, and Mrs. Geldard was astonished to find folded and laid on a cupboard shelf the entire suit of clothes that her husband had worn when he left home on the morning of the previous day. She also found in the waste paper basket the fragments of two or three envelopes addressed to her husband, which she brought for Hewitt's inspection. They were in the handwriting of the girl Trennatt, and with them Mrs. Geldard had discovered a small fragment of one of the letters, a mere scrap, but sufficient to show part of the signature "Emma," and two or three of a row of crosses running beneath, such as are employed to represent kisses. These things she had brought with her.

Hewitt examined them slightly and then asked, "Can I have a photograph of your husband, Mrs. Geldard?"

She immediately produced, not only a photograph of her husband, but also one of the girl Trennatt, which she said belonged to the cook. Hewitt complimented her on her foresight. "And now," he said, "I think we'll go and take a look at Mr. Geldard's office, if we may. Of course I shall follow him up now." Hewitt made a sign to me, which I interpreted as asking whether I would care to accompany him. I assented with a nod, for the case seemed likely to be interesting.

I omit most of Mrs. Geldard's talk by the way, which was almost ceaseless, mostly compounded of useless repetition, and very tiresome.

The office was on a third floor in a large building in Finsbury Pavement. The caretaker made no difficulty in admitting us. There were two rooms, neither very large, and one of them at the back very small indeed. In this was a small locked door.

"That leads on to the small staircase, sir," the caretaker said in response to Hewitt's inquiry. "The staircase leads down to the basement, and it ain't used much 'cept by the cleaners."

"If I went down this back staircase," Hewitt pursued, "I suppose I should have no difficulty in gaining the street?"

"Not a bit, sir. You'd have to go a little way round to get into Finsbury Pavement, but there's a passage leads straight from the bottom of the stairs out to Moorfields behind."

"Yes," remarked Mrs. Geldard bitterly, when the caretaker had left the room, "that's the way he's been leaving the office every day, and in disguise, too." She pointed to the cupboard where her husband's clothes lay. "Pretty plain proof that he was ashamed of his doings, whatever they were."

"Come, come," Hewitt answered deprecatingly, "we'll hope there's nothing to be ashamed of—at any rate till there's proof of it. There's no proof as yet that your husband has been disguising. A great many men who rent offices, I believe, keep dress clothes at them—I do it myself—for convenience in case of an unexpected invitation, or such other eventuality. We may find that he returned here last night, put on his evening dress and went somewhere dining. Illness, or fifty accidents, may have kept him from home."

But Mrs. Geldard was not to be softened by any such suggestion, which I could see Hewitt bad chiefly thrown out by way of pacifying the lady, and allaying her bitterness as far as he could, in view of a possible reconciliation when things were cleared up.

"That isn't very likely," she said. "If he kept a dress suit here openly I should know of it, and if he kept it here unknown to me, what did he want it for? If he went out in dress clothes last night, who did he go with? Who do you suppose, after seeing those envelopes and that piece of the letter?"

"Well, well, we shall see," Hewitt replied. "May I turn out the pockets of these clothes?"

"Certainly; there's nothing in them of importance," Mrs. Geldard said. "I looked before I came to you."

Nevertheless Hewitt turned them out. "Here is a cheque-book with a number of cheques remaining. No counterfoils filled in, which is awkward. Bankers, the London Amalgamated. We will call there presently. An ivory pocket paper-knife. A sovereign purse—empty." Hewitt placed the articles on the table as he named them. "Gold pencil case, ivory folding rule, russia-leather card-case." He turned to Mrs. Geldard. "There is no pocket-book," he said, "no pocket-knife and no watch, and there are no keys. Did Mr. Geldard usually carry any of these things?"

"Yes," Mrs. Geldard replied, "he carried all four." Hewitt's simple methodical calmness, and his plain disregard of her former volubility, appeared by this to have disciplined Mrs. Geldard into a businesslike brevity and directness of utterance.

"As to the watch now. Can you describe it?"

"Oh, it was only a cheap one. He had a gold one stolen—or at any rate he told me so—and since then he has only carried a very common sort of silver one, without a chain."

"The keys?"

"I only know there was a bunch of keys. Some of them fitted drawers and bureaux at home, and others, I suppose, fitted locks in this office."

"What of the pocket-knife?"

"That was a very uncommon one. It was a present, as a matter of fact, from an engineering friend, who had had it made specially. It was large, with a tortoise-shell handle and a silver plate with his initials. There was only one ordinary knife-blade in it, all the other implements were small tools or things of that kind. There was a small pair of silver calipers, for instance."

"Like these?" Hewitt suggested, producing those he used for measuring drawers and cabinets in search of secret receptacles.

"Yes, like those. And there were folding steel compasses, a tiny flat spanner, a little spirit level, and a number of other small instruments of that sort. It was very well made indeed; he used to say that it could not have been made for five pounds."

"Indeed?" Hewitt cast his eyes about the two rooms. "I see no signs of books here, Mrs. Geldard—account books I mean, of course. Your husband must have kept account books, I take it?"

"Yes, naturally; he must have done. I never saw them, of course, but every business man keeps books." Then after a pause Mrs. Geldard continued: "And they're gone too. I never thought of that. But there, I might have known as much. Who can trust a man safely if his own wife can't? But I won't shield him. Whatever he's been doing with his clients' money he'll have to answer for himself. Thank heaven I've enough to live on of my own without being dependent on a creature like him But think of the disgrace! My husband nothing better than a common thief—swindling his clients and making away with his books when he can't go on any longer! But he shall be punished, oh yes; I'll see he's punished, if once I find him!"

Hewitt thought for a moment, and then asked: "Do you know any of your husband's clients, Mrs. Geldard?"

"No," she answered, rather snappishly, "I don't. I've told you he never let me know anything of his business—never anything at all; and very good reason he had too, that's certain."

"Then probably you do not happen to know the contents of these drawers?" Hewitt pursued, tapping the writing-table as he spoke.

"Oh, there's nothing of importance in them—at any rate in the unlocked ones. I looked at all of them this morning when I first came."

The table was of the ordinary pedestal pattern with four drawers at each side and a ninth in the middle at the top, and of very ordinary quality. The only locked drawer was the third from the top on the left-hand side. Hewitt pulled out one drawer after another. In one was a tin half full of tobacco; in another a few cigars at the bottom of a box; in a third a pile of notepaper headed with the address of the office, and rather dusty; another was empty; still another contained a handful of string. The top middle drawer rather reminded me of a similar drawer of my own at my last newspaper office, for it contained several pipes; but my own were mostly briars, whereas these were all clays.

"There's nothing really so satisfactory," Hewitt said, as he lifted and examined each pipe by turn, "to a seasoned smoker as a well-used clay. Most such men keep one or more such pipes for strictly private use." There was nothing noticeable about these pipes except that they were uncommonly dirty, but Hewitt scrutinised each before returning it to the drawer. Then he turned to Mrs. Geldard and said: "As to the bank now—the London Amalgamated, Mrs. Geldard. Are you known there personally?"

"Oh, yes; my husband gave them authority to pay cheques signed by me up to a certain amount, and I often do it for household expenses, or when he happens to be away."

"Then perhaps it will be best for you to go alone," Hewitt responded. "Of course they will never, as a general thing, give any person information as to the account of a customer, but perhaps, as you are known to them, and hold your husband's authority to draw cheques, they may tell you something. What I want to find out is, of course, whether your husband drew from the bank all his remaining balance yesterday, or any large sum. You must go alone, ask for the manager, and tell him that you have seen nothing of Mr. Geldard since he left for business yesterday morning. Mind, you are not to appear angry, or suspicious, or anything of that sort, and you mustn't say you are employing me to bring him back from an elopement. That will shut up the channel of information at once. Hostile inquiries they'll never answer, even by the smallest hint, except after legal injunction. You can be as distressed and as alarmed as you please. Your husband has disappeared since yesterday morning, and you've no notion what has become of him; that is your tale, and a perfectly true one. You would like to know whether or not he has withdrawn his balance, or a considerable sum, since that would indicate whether or not his absence was intentional and premeditated."

Mrs. Geldard understood and undertook to make the inquiry with all discretion. The bank was not far, and it was arranged that she should return to the office with the result.

As soon as she had left Hewitt turned to the pedestal table and probed the keyhole of the locked drawer with the small stiletto attached to his penknife. "This seems to be a common sort of lock," he said. "I could probably open it with a bent nail. But the whole table is a cheap sort of thing. Perhaps there is an easier way."

He drew the unlocked drawer above completely out, passed his hand into the opening and felt about. "Yes," he said, "it's just as I hoped—as it usually is in pedestal tables not of the best quality; the partition between the drawers doesn't go more than two-thirds of the way back, and I can drop my hand into the drawer below. But T can't feel anything there—it seems empty."

He withdrew his hand and we tilted the whole table backward, so as to cause whatever lay in the drawers to slide to the back. This dodge was successful. Hewitt reinserted his hand and withdrew it with two orderly heaps of papers, each held together by a metal clip.

The papers in each clip, on examination, proved to be all of an identical character, with the exception of dates. They were, in fact, rent receipts. Those for the office, which had been given quarterly, were put back in their place with scarcely a glance, and the others Hewitt placed on the table before him. Each ran, apart from dates, in this fashion: "Received from Mr. J. Cookson 15s., one month's rent of stable at 8 Dragon Yard, Benton Street, to"—here followed the date. "Also rent, feed and care of horse in own stable as agreed, £2.—W. GASK." The receipts were ill-written, and here and there ill-spelt. Hewitt put the last of the receipts in his pocket and returned the others to the drawer. "Either," he said, "Mr. Cookson is a client who gets Mr. Geldard to hire stables for him, which may not be likely, or Mr. Geldard calls himself Mr. Cookson when he goes driving—possibly with Miss Trennatt. We shall see."

The pedestal table put in order again, Hewitt took the poker and raked in the fireplace. It was summer, and behind the bars was a sort of screen of cartridge paper with a frilled edge, and behind this various odds and ends had been thrown—spent matches, trade-circulars crumpled up, and torn paper. There were also the remains of several cigars, some only half smoked, and one almost whole. The torn paper Hewitt examined piece by piece, and finally sorted out a number of pieces which he set to work to arrange on the blotting pad. They formed a complete note, written in the same hand as were the envelopes already found by Mrs. Geldard—that of the girl Emma Trennatt. It corresponded also with the solitary fragment of another letter which had accompanied them, by way of having a number of crosses below the signature, and it ran thus:—

Tuesday Night.

Dear Sam,—To-morrow, to carry. Not late because people are coming for flowers. What you did was no good. The smoke leaks worse than ever, and F. thinks you must light a new pipe or else stop smoking altogether for a bit. Uncle is anxious.—Emma.

Then followed the crosses, filling one line and nearly half the next; seventeen in all.

Hewitt gazed at the fragments thoughtfully. "This is a find," he said—"most decidedly a find. It looks so much like nonsense that it must mean something of importance. The date, you see, is Tuesday night. It would be received here on Wednesday—yesterday—morning. So that it was immediately after the receipt of this note that Geldard left. It's pretty plain the crosses don't mean kisses. The note isn't quite of the sort that usually carries such symbols, and moreover, when a lady fills the end of a sheet of notepaper with kisses she doesn't stop less than half way across the last line—she fills it to the end. These crosses mean something very different. I should like, too, to know what 'smoke' means. Anyway this letter would probably astonish Mrs. Geldard if she saw it. We'll say nothing about it for the present." He swept the fragments into an envelope, and put away the envelope in his breast pocket. There was nothing more to be found of the least value in the fireplace, and a careful examination of the office in other parts revealed nothing that I had not noticed before, so far as I could see, except Geldard's boots standing on the floor of the cupboard wherein his clothes lay. The whole place was singularly bare of what one commonly finds in an office in the way of papers, handbooks, and general business material.

Mrs. Geldard was not long away. At the bank she found that the manager was absent and his deputy had been very reluctant to say anything definite without his sanction. He gave Mrs. Geldard to understand, however, that there was a balance still remaining to her husband's credit; also that Mr. Geldard had drawn a cheque the previous morning, Wednesday, for an amount "rather larger than usual." And that was all.

"By the way, Mrs. Geldard," Hewitt observed, with an air of recollecting something, "there was a Mr. Cookson I believe, if I remember, who knew a Mr. Geldard. You don't happen to know, do you, whether or not Mr. Geldard had a client or an acquaintance of that name?"

"No, I know nobody of the name."

"Ah, it doesn't matter. I suppose it isn't necessary for your husband to keep horses or vehicles of any description in his business?"

"No, certainly not." Mrs. Geldard looked surprised at the question.

"Of course—I should have known that. He does not drive to business, I suppose?"

"No, he goes by omnibus."

"But as to Emma Trennatt now. This photograph is most welcome, and will be of great assistance, I make no doubt. But is there anything individual by which I might identify her if I saw her—anything beyond what I see in the photograph? A peculiarity of step, for instance, or a scar, or what not."

"Yes, there is a large mole—more than a quarter of an inch across I should think—on her left cheek, an inch below the outer corner of her eye. The photograph only shows the other side of the face."

"That will be useful to know. Now has she a relative living at Crouch End, or thereabout?"

"Yes, her uncle; she's living with him now—or she was at any rate till lately. But how did you know that?"

"The Crouch End postmark was on those envelopes you found. Do you know anything of her uncle?"

"Nothing, except that he's a nurseryman, I believe."

"Not his full address?"

"No."

"And Trennatt is his name?"

"Thank you. I think, Mrs. Geldard," Hewitt said, taking his hat, "that I will set out after your husband at once. You, I think, can do no better than stay at home till I have news for you. I have your address. If anything comes to your knowledge please telegraph it to my office at once."

The office door was locked, the keys were left with the caretaker, and we saw Mrs. Geldard into a cab at the door. "Come," said Hewitt, "we'll go somewhere and look at a directory, and after that to Dragon Yard. I think I know a man in Moorgate Street who'll let me see his directory."

We started to walk down Finsbury Pavement. Suddenly Hewitt caught my arm and directed my eyes toward a woman who had passed hurriedly in the opposite direction. I had not seen her face, but Hewitt had. "If that isn't Miss Emma Trennatt," he said, "it's uncommonly like the notion I've formed of her. We'll see if she goes to Geldard's office."

We hurried after the woman, who, sure enough, turned into the large door of the building we had just left. As it was impossible that she should know us we followed her boldly up the stairs and saw her stop before the door of Geldard's office and knock. We passed her as she stood there—a handsome young woman enough—and well back on her left cheek, in the place Mrs. Geldard had indicated, there was plain to see a very large mole. We pursued our way to the landing above and there we stopped in a position that commanded a view of Geldard's door. The young woman knocked again and waited.

"This doesn't look like an elopement yesterday morning, does it?" Hewitt whispered. "Unless Geldard's left both this one and his wife in the lurch."

The young woman below knocked once or twice more, walked irresolutely across the corridor and back, and in the end, after a parting knock, started slowly back downstairs.

"Brett," Hewitt exclaimed with suddenness, "will you do me a favour? That woman understands Geldard's secret comings and goings, as is plain from the letter. But she would appear to know nothing of where he is now, since she seems to have come here to find him. Perhaps this last absence of his has nothing to do with the others. In any case will you follow this woman? She must be watched; but I want to see to the matter in other places. Will you do it?"

Of course I assented at once. We had been descending the stairs as Hewitt spoke, keeping distance behind the girl we were following. "Thank you," Hewitt now said. "Do it. If you find anything urgent to communicate wire to me in care of the inspector at Crouch End Police Station. He knows me, and I will call there in case you may have sent. But if it's after five this afternoon, wire also to my office. If you keep with her to Crouch End, where she lives, we shall probably meet."

We parted at the door of the office we were at first bound for, and I followed the girl southward.

This new turn of affairs increased the puzzlement I already laboured under. Here was the girl Trennatt—who by all evidence appeared to be well acquainted with Geldard's mysterious proceedings, and in consequence of whose letter, whatever it might mean, he would seem to have absented himself—herself apparently ignorant of his whereabouts and even unconscious that he had left his office. I had at first begun to speculate on Geldard's probable secret employment; I had heard of men keeping good establishments who, unknown to even their own wives, procured the wherewithal by begging or crossing-sweeping in London streets; I had heard also—knew in fact from Hewitt's experience—of well-to-do suburban residents whose actual profession was burglary or coining. I had speculated on the possibility of Geldard's secret being one of that kind. My mind had even reverted to the case, which I have related elsewhere, in which Hewitt frustrated a dynamite explosion by his timely discovery of a baker's cart and a number of loaves, and I wondered whether or not Geldard was a member of some secret brotherhood of Anarchists or Fenians. But here, it would seem, were two distinct mysteries, one of Geldard's generally unaccountable movements, and another of his disappearance, each mystery complicating the other. Again, what did that extraordinary note mean, with its crosses and its odd references to smoking? Had the dirty clay pipes anything to do with it? Or the half-smoked cigars? Perhaps the whole thing was merely ridiculously trivial after all. I could make nothing of it, however, and applied myself to my pursuit of Emma Trennatt, who mounted an omnibus at the Bank, on the roof of which I myself secured a seat.

II

Here I must leave my own proceedings to put in their proper place those of Martin Hewitt as I subsequently learnt them.

Benton Street, he found by the directory, turned out of the City Road south of Old Street, so was quite near. He was there in less than ten minutes, and had discovered Dragon Yard. Dragon Yard was as small a stable-yard as one could easily find. Only the right-hand side was occupied by stables, and there were only three of these. On the left was a high dead wall bounding a great warehouse or some such building. Across the first and second of the stables stretched a long board with the legend, "W. Gask, Corn, Hay and Straw Dealer," and underneath a shop address in Old Street. The third stable stood blank and uninscribed, and all three were shut fast. Nobody was in the yard, and Hewitt at once proceeded to examine the end stable. The doors were unusually well finished and close-fitting, and the lock was a good one, of the lever variety, and very difficult to pick. Hewitt examined the front of the building very carefully, and then, after a visit to the entrance of the yard, to guard against early interruption, returned and scrambled by projections and fastenings to the roof. This was a roof in contrast to those of the other stables. They were of tiles, seemed old, and carried nothing in the way of a skylight; evidently it was the habit of Mr. Gask and his helpers to do their horse and van business with gates wide open to admit light. But the roof of this third stable was newer and better made, and carried a good-sized skylight of thick fluted glass. Hewitt took a good look at such few windows as happened to be in sight, and straight away began, with the strongest blade of his pocket-knife, to cut away the putty from round one pane. It was a rather long job, for the putty had hardened thoroughly in the sun, but it was accomplished at length, and Hewitt, with a final glance at the windows in view, prized up the pane from the end and lifted it out.

The interior of the stable was apparently empty. Neither stall nor rack was to be seen; and the place was plainly used as a coach or van house simply. Hewitt took one more look about him and dropped quietly through the hole in the skylight. The floor was thickly laid with straw. There were a few odd pieces of harness, a rope or two, a lantern, and a few sacks lying here and there, and at the darkest end there was, an obscure heap covered with straw and sacking. This heap Hewitt proceeded to unmask, and having cleared away a few sacks left revealed about half-a-dozen rolls of linoleum. One of these he dragged to the light, where it became evident that it had remained thus rolled and tied with cord in two places for a long period. There were cracks in the surface, and when the cords were loosened the linoleum showed no disposition to open out or to become unrolled. Others of the rolls on inspection exhibited the same peculiarities. Moreover, each roll appeared to consist of no more than a couple of yards of material at most, though all were of the same pattern. Every roll in fact was of the same length, thickness and shape as the others, containing somewhere near two yards of linoleum in a roll of some half dozen thicknesses, leaving an open diameter of some four inches in the centre. Hewitt looked at each in turn and then replaced the heap as he had found it. After this to regain the skylight was not difficult by the aid of a trestle. The pane was replaced as well as the absence of fresh putty permitted, and five minutes later Hewitt was in a hansom bound for Crouch End.

He dismissed his cab at the police station. Within he had no difficulty in procuring a direction to Trennatt, the nurseryman, and a short walk brought him to the place. A fairly high wall topped with broken glass bounded the nursery garden next the road and in the wall were two gates, one a wide double one for the admission of vehicles, and the other a smaller one of open pales, for ordinary visitors. The garden stood sheltered by higher ground behind, whereon stood a good-sized house, just visible among the trees that surrounded it. Hewitt walked along by the side of the wall. Soon he came to where the ground of the nursery garden appeared to be divided from that of the house by a most extraordinarily high hedge extending a couple of feet above the top of the wall itself. Stepping back, the better to note this hedge, Hewitt became conscious of two large boards, directly facing each other, with scarcely four feet space between them, one erected on a post in the ground of the house and the other similarly elevated from that of the nursery, each being inscribed in large letters, "Trespassers will be prosecuted."

Hewitt smiled and passed on; here plainly was a neighbour's quarrel of long standing, for neither board was by any means new. The wall continued, and keeping by it Hewitt made the entire circuit of the large house and its grounds, and arrived once more at that part of the wall that enclosed the nursery garden. Just here, and near the wider gate, the upper part of a cottage was visible, standing within the wall, and evidently the residence of the nurseryman. It carried a conspicuous board with the legend, "H. M. Trennatt, Nurseryman." The large house and the nursery stood entirely apart from other houses or enclosures, and it would seem that the nursery ground had at some time been cut off from the grounds attached to the house.

Hewitt stood for a moment thoughtfully, and then walked back to the outer gate of the house on the rise. It was a high iron gate, and as Hewitt perceived, it was bolted at the bottom. Within the garden showed a neglected and weed-choked appearance, such as one associates with the garden of a house that has stood long empty.

A little way off a policeman walked. Hewitt accosted him and spoke of the house. "I was wondering if it might happen to be to let," he said. "Do you know?"

"No, sir," the policeman replied, "it ain't; though anyone might almost think it, to look at the garden. That's a Mr. Fuller as lives there—and a rum 'un too."

"Oh, he's a rum 'un, is he? Keeps himself shut up, perhaps?"

"Yes, sir. On'y 'as one old woman, deaf as a post, for servant, and never lets nobody into the place. It's a rare game sometimes with the milkman. The milkman, he comes and rings that there bell, but the old gal's so deaf she never 'ears it. Then the milkman, he just slips 'is 'and through the gate-rails, lifts the bolt and goes and bangs at the door. Old Fuller runs out and swears a good 'un. The old gal comes out and old Fuller swears at 'er, and she turns round and swears back like anything. She don't care for 'im—not a bit. Then when he ain't 'avin' a row with the milkman and the old gal he goes down the garden and rows with the old nurseryman there down the 'ill. He jores the nurseryman from 'is side o' the hedge and the nurseryman he jores back at the top of 'is voice. I've stood out there ten minutes together and nearly bust myself a-laughin' at them gray-'eaded old fellers a-callin' each other everythink they can think of; you can 'ear 'em 'alf over the parish. Why, each of 'em's 'ad a board painted, 'Trespassers will be Prosecuted,' and stuck 'em up facin' each other, so as to keep up the row."

"Very funny, no doubt."

"Funny? I believe you, sir. Why it's quite a treat sometimes on a dull beat like this. Why, what's that? slowed if I don't think they're beginning again now. Yes, they are. Well, my beat's the other way."

There was a sound of angry voices in the direction of the nursery ground, and Hewitt made toward it. Just where the hedge peeped over the wall the altercation was plain to hear.

"You're an old vagabond, and I'll indict you for a nuisance!"

"You're an old thief, and you'd like to turn me out of house and home, wouldn't you? Indict away, you greedy old scoundrel!"

These and similar endearments, punctuated by growls and snorts, came distinctly from over the wall, accompanied by a certain scraping, brushing sound, as though each neighbour were madly attempting to scale the hedge and personally bang the other.

Hewitt hastened round to the front of the nursery garden and quietly tried first the wide gate and next the small one. Both were fastened securely. But in the manner of the milkman at the gate of the house above, Hewitt slipped his hand between the open slats of the small gate and slid the night-latch that held it. Within the quarrel ran high as Hewitt stepped quietly into the garden. He trod on the narrow grass borders of the beds for quietness' sake, till presently only a line of shrubs divided him from the clamorous nurseryman. Stooping and looking through an opening which gave him a back view, Hewitt observed that the brushing and scraping noise proceeded, not from angry scramblings, but from the forcing through an inadequate opening in the hedge of some piece of machinery which the nurseryman was most amicably passing to his neighbour at the same time as he assailed him with savage abuse, and received a full return in kind. It appeared to consist of a number of coils of metal pipe, not unlike those sometimes used in heating apparatus, and was as yet only a very little way through. Something else, of bright copper, lay on the garden-bed at the foot of the hedge, but intervening plants concealed its shape.

Hewitt turned quickly away and made towards the greenhouses, keeping tall shrubs as much as possible between himself and the cottage, and looking sharply about him. Here and there about the garden were stand-pipes, each carrying a tap at its upper end and placed conveniently for irrigation. These in particular Hewitt scrutinised, and presently, as he neared a large wooden outhouse close by the large gate, turned his attention to one backed by a thick shrub. When the thick undergrowth of the shrub was pushed aside a small stone slab, black and dirty, was disclosed, and this Hewitt lifted, uncovering a square hole six or eight inches across, from the fore-side of which the stand-pipe rose.

The row went cheerily on over by the hedge, and neither Trennatt nor his neighbour saw Hewitt, feeling with his hand, discover two stop-cocks and a branch pipe in the hole, nor saw him try them both. Hewitt, however, was satisfied, and saw his case plain. He rose and made his way back toward the small gate. He was scarce half-way there when the straining of the hedge ceased, and before he reached it the last insult had been hurled, the quarrel ceased, and Trennatt approached. Hewitt immediately turned his back to the gate, and looking about him inquiringly hemmed aloud as though to attract attention. The nurseryman promptly burst round a corner crying, "Who's that? who's that, eh? What d'ye want, eh?"

"Why," answered Hewitt in a tone of mild surprise, "is it so uncommon to have a customer drop in?"

"I'd ha' sworn that gate was fastened," the old man said, looking about him suspiciously.

"That would have been rash; I had no difficulty in opening it. Come, can't you sell me a button-hole?"

The old man led the way to a greenhouse, but as he went he growled again, "I'd ha' sworn I shut that gate."

"Perhaps you forgot," Hewitt suggested. "You have had a little excitement with your neighbour, haven't you?"

Trennatt stopped and turned round, darting a keen glance into Hewitt's face.

"Yes," he answered angrily, "I have. He's an old villain. He'd like to turn me out of here, after being here all my life-and a lot o' good the ground 'ud be to him if he kep' it like he keeps his own! And look there!" He dragged Hewitt toward the "Trespassers" boards. "Goes and sticks up a board like that looking over my hedge! As though I wanted to go over among his weeds! So I stuck up another in front of it, and now they can stare each other out o' countenance. Buttonhole, you said, sir, eh?"

The old man saw Hewitt off the premises with great care, and the latter, flower in coat, made straight for the nearest post-office and despatched a telegram. Then he stood for some little while outside the post-office deep in thought, and in the end returned to the gate of the house above the nursery.

With much circumspection he opened the gate and entered the grounds. But instead of approaching the house he turned immediately to the left, behind trees and shrubs, making for the side nearest the nursery.

Soon he reached a long, low wooden shed.

The door was only secured by a button, and turning this he gazed into the dark interior.

Now he had not noticed that close after him a woman had entered the gate, and that that woman was Mrs. Geldard. She would have made for the house, but catching sight of Hewitt, followed him swiftly and quietly over the long grass. Thus it came to pass that his first apprisal of the lady's presence was a sharp drive in the back which pitched him down the step to the low floor of what he had just perceived to be merely a tool-house, after which the door was shut and buttoned behind him.

"Perhaps you'll be more careful in future," game Mrs. Geldard's angry voice from without, "how you go making mischief between husband and wife and poking your nose into people's affairs. Such fellows as you ought to be well punished."

Hewitt laughed softly. Mrs. Geldard had evidently changed her mind. The door presented no difficulty; a fairly vigorous push dislodged the button entirely, and he walked back to the outer gate chuckling quietly. In the distance he heard Mrs. Geldard in shrill altercation with the deaf old woman. "It's no good you a-talking," the old woman was saying. "I can't hear. Nobody ain't allowed in this here place, so you must get out. Out you go now!" Outside the gate Hewitt met me.

III

My own adventure had been simple. I had secured a back seat on the roof of the omnibus whereon Emma Trennatt travelled south from the Bank, from which I could easily observe where she alighted. When she did so I followed, and found to my astonishment that her destination was no other than the Geldards' private house at Camberwell—as I remembered from the address on the visitor's slip which Mrs. Geldard had handed in at Hewitt's office a couple of days before. She handed a letter to the maid who opened the door, and soon after, in response to a message by the same maid, entered the house. Presently the maid reappeared, bonneted, and hurried off, to return in a few minutes in a cab with another following behind.

Almost immediately Mrs. Geldard emerged in company with Emma Trennatt. She hurried the girl into one of the cabs, and I heard her repeat loudly twice the address of Hewitt's office, once to the girl and once to the cabman. Now it seemed plain to me that to follow Emma Trennatt farther would be waste of time, for she was off to Hewitt's office, where Kerrett would learn her message. And knowing where a message would find Hewitt sooner than at his office, I judged it well to tell Mrs. Geldard of the fact. I approached, therefore, as she was entering the other cab and began to explain when she cut me short.

"You go and tell your master to attend to his own business as soon as he pleases, for not a shilling does he get from me. He ought to be ashamed of himself, sowing dissension between man and wife for the sake of what he can make out of it, and so ought you."

I bowed with what grace I might, and retired. The other cab had gone, so I set forth to find one for myself at the nearest rank. I could think of nothing better to do than to make for Crouch End Police Station and endeavour to find Hewitt. Soon after my cab emerged north of the city I became conscious of another cab whose driver I fancied I recognised, and which kept ahead all along the route. In fact it was Mrs. Geldard's cab, and presently it dawned upon him that we must both be bound for the same place. When it became quite clear that Crouch End was the destination of the lady I instructed my driver to disregard the police station and follow the cab in front. Thus I arrived at Mr. Fuller's house just behind Mrs. Geldard, and thus, waiting at the gate, I met Hewitt as he emerged.

"Hullo, Brett!" he said. "Condole with me. Mrs. Geldard has changed her mind, and considers me a pernicious creature anxious to make mischief between her and her husband; I'm very much afraid I shan't get my fee."

"No," I answered, "she told me you wouldn't."

We compared notes, and Hewitt laughed heartily. "The appearance of Emma Trennatt at Geldard's office this morning is explained," he said. "She went first with a message from Geldard to Mrs. Geldard at Camberwell, explaining his absence and imploring her not to talk of it or make a disturbance. Mrs. Geldard had gone off to town, and Emma Trennatt was told that she had gone to Geldard's office. There she went, and then we first saw her. She found nobody at the office, and after a minute or two of irresolution returned to Camberwell, and then succeeded in delivering her message, as you saw. Mrs. Geldard is apparently satisfied with her husband's explanation. But I'm afraid the revenue officers won't approve of it."

"The revenue officers?"

"Yes. It's a case of illicit distilling—and a big case, I fancy. I've wired to Somerset House, and no doubt men are on their way here now. But Mrs. Geldard's up at the house, so we'd better hurry up to the police station and have a few sent from there. Come along. The whole thing's very clever, and a most uncommonly big thing. If I know all about it—and I think I do—Geldard and his partners have been turning out untaxed spirit by the hundred gallons for a long time past. Geldard is the practical man, the engineer, and probably erected the whole apparatus himself in that house on the hill. The spirit is brought down by a pipe laid a very little way under the garden surface, and carried into one of the irrigation stand-pipes in the nursery ground. There's a quiet little hole behind the pipe with a couple of stop-cocks—one to shut off the water when necessary, the other to do the same with the spirit. When the stopcocks are right you just turn the tap at the top of the pipe and you get water or whisky, as the case may be. Fuller, the man up at the house, attends to the still, with such assistance as the deaf old woman can give him. Trennatt, down below, draws off the liquor ready to be carried away. These two keep up an ostentatious appearance of being at unending feud to blind suspicion. Our as yet ungreeted friend Geldard, guiding spirit of the whole thing, comes disguised as a carter with an apparent cart-load of linoleum, and carries away the manufactured stuff. In the pleasing language of Geldard and Co., 'smoke,' as alluded to in the note you saw, means whisky. Something has been wrong with the apparatus lately, and it has been leaking badly. Geldard has been at work on it, patching, but ineffectually. 'What you did was no good' said the charming Emma in the note, as you will remember. 'Uncle was anxious.' And justifiably so, because not only does a leak of spirit mean a waste, but it means a smell, which some sharp revenue man might sniff. Moreover, if there is a leak, the liquid runs somewhere at random, and with any sudden increase in volume attention might easily be attracted. It was so bad that 'F.' (Fuller) thought Geldard must light another pipe (start another still) or give up smoking (distilling) for a bit. There is the explanation of the note. 'To-morrow, to carry' probably means that he is to call with his cart—the cart in whose society Geldard becomes Cookson—to remove a quantity of spirit. He is not to come late because people are expected on floral business. The crosses I think will be found to indicate the amount of liquid to be moved. But that we shall see. Anyhow Geldard got there yesterday and had a busy day loading up, and then set to repairing. The damage was worse than supposed, and an urgent thing. Result, Geldard works into early morning, has a sleep in the place, where he may be called at any moment, and starts again early this morning. New parts have to be ordered, and these are delivered at Trennatt's to-day and passed through the hedge. Meantime Geldard sends a message to his wife explaining things, and the result you've seen."

At the police station a telegram had already been received from Somerset House. That was enough for Hewitt, who had discharged his duty as a citizen and now dropped the case. We left the police and the revenue officers to deal with the matter and travelled back to town.

"Yes," said Hewitt on the way, after each had fully described his day's experiences, "it seemed pretty plain that Geldard left his office by the back way in disguise, and there were things that hinted what that disguise was. The pipes were noticeable. They were quite unnecessarily dirty, and partly from dirty fingers. Pipes smoked by a man in his office would never look like that. They had been smoked out of doors by a man with dirty hands, and hands and pipes would be in keeping with the rest of the man's appearance. It was noticeable that he had left not only his clothes and hat but his boots behind him. They were quite plain though good boots, and would be quite in keeping with any dress but that of a labourer or some such man in his working clothes. Moreover the partly-smoked cigars were probably thrown aside because they would appear inconsistent with Geldard's changed dress. The contents of the pockets in the clothes left behind, too, told the same tale. The cheap watch and the necessary keys, pocketbook and pocket-knife were taken, but the articles of luxury, the russia-leather card-case, the sovereign purse and so on were left. Then we came on the receipts for stable-rent. Suggestion—perhaps the disguise was that of a carter.

"Then there was the coach-house. Plainly, if Geldard took the trouble thus to disguise himself, and thus to hide his occupation even from his wife, he had sonic very good reason for secrecy. Now the goods which a man would be likely to carry secretly in a cart or van, as a regular piece of business, would probably be either stolen or smuggled. When I examined those pieces of linoleum I became convinced that they were intended merely as receptacles for some other sort of article altogether. They were old, and had evidently been thus rolled for a very long period. They appeared to have been exposed to weather, but on the outside only. Moreover they were all of one size and shape, each forming a long hollow cylinder, with plenty of interior room. Now from this it was plainly unlikely that they were intended to hold stolen goods.

"Stolen goods are not apt to be always of one size and shape, adaptable to a cylindrical recess. Perhaps they were smuggled. Now the only goods profitable to be smuggled nowadays are tobacco and spirits, and plainly these rolls of linoleum would be excellent receptacles for either. Tobacco could be packed inside the rolls and the ends stopped artistically with narrow rolls of linoleum. Spirits could be contained in metal cylinders exactly fitting the cavity and the ends filled in the same way as for tobacco. But for tobacco a smart man would probably make his linoleum rolls of different sizes, for the sake of a more innocent appearance, while for spirits it would be a convenience to have vessels of uniform measure, to save trouble in quicker delivery and calculation of quantity. Bearing these things in mind I went in search of the gentle nurseryman at Crouch End. My general survey of the nursery ground and the house behind it inspired me with the notion that the situation and arrangement were most admirably adapted for the working of a large illicit still—a form of misdemeanour, let me tell you, that is much more common nowadays than is generally supposed. I remembered Geldard's engineering experience, and I heard something of the odd manners of Mr. Puller; my theory of a traffic in untaxed spirits became strengthened. But why a nursery? Was this a mere accident of the design? There were commonly irrigation pipes about nurseries, and an extra one might easily be made to carry whisky. With this in mind I visited the nursery with the result you know of. The stand-pipe I tested (which was where I expected—handy to the vehicle-entrance) could produce simple New River water or raw whisky at command of one of two stop-cocks. My duty was plain. As you know, I am a citizen first and an investigator after, and I find the advantage of it in my frequent intercourse with the police and other authorities. As soon as I could get away I telegraphed to Somerset House. But then I grew perplexed on a point of conduct. I was commissioned by Mrs. Geldard. It scarcely seemed the loyal thing to put my client's husband in gaol because of what I had learnt in course of work on her behalf. I decided to give him, and nobody else, a sporting chance. If I could possibly get at him in the time at my disposal, by himself, so that no accomplice should get the benefit of my warning, I would give him a plain hint to run; then he could take his chance. I returned to the place and began to work round the grounds, examining the place as I went; but at the very first outhouse I put my head into I was surprised in the rear by Mrs. Geldard coming in hot haste to stop me and rescue her husband. She most unmistakably gave me the sack, and so now the police may catch Geldard or not, as their luck may be."

They did catch him. In the next day's papers a report of a great capture of illicit distillers occupied a prominent place. The prisoners were James Fuller, Henry Matthew Trennatt, Sarah Blatten, a deaf woman, Samuel Geldard and his wife Rebecca Geldard. The two women were found on the premises in violent altercation when the officers arrived, a few minutes after Hewitt and I had left the police station on our way home. It was considered by far the greatest haul for the revenue authorities since the seizure of the famous ship's boiler on a waggon in the East-End stuffed full of tobacco, after that same ship's boiler had made about a dozen voyages to the continent and back "for repair." Geldard was found dressed as a workman, carrying out extensive alterations and repairs to the still. And a light van was found in a shed belonging to the nursery loaded with seventeen rolls of linoleum, each enclosing a cylinder containing two gallons of spirits, and packed at each end with narrow linoleum rolls. It will be remembered that seventeen was the number of crosses at the foot of Emma Trennatt's note.

The subsequent raids on a number of obscure public-houses in different parts of London, in consequence of information gathered on the occasion of the Geldard capture, resulted in the seizure of a large quantity of secreted spirit for which no permit could be shown. It demonstrated also the extent of Geldard's connection, and indicated plainly what was done with the spirit when he had carted it away from Crouch End. Some of the public-houses in question must have acquired a notoriety among the neighbours for frequent purchases of linoleum.

III. — THE CASE OF THE DEAD SKIPPER

I

It is a good few years ago now that a suicide was investigated by a coroner's jury, before whom Martin Hewitt gave certain simple and direct evidence touching the manner of the death, and testifying to the fact of its being a matter of self-destruction. The public got certain suggestive information from the bare newspaper report, but they never learnt the full story of the tragedy that led up to the suicide that was so summarily disposed of.

The time I speak of was in Hewitt's early professional days, not long after he had left Messrs. Crellan's office, and a long time before I myself met him. At that time fewer of the police knew him and were aware of his abilities, and fewer still appreciated them at their true value. Inquiries in connection with a case had taken him early one morning to the district which is now called "London over the border," and which comprises West Ham and the parts there adjoining. At this time, however, the district was much unlike its present self, for none of the grimy streets that now characterise it had been built, and even in its nearest parts open laud claimed more space than buildings.

Hewitt's business lay with the divisional surgeon of police, who had, he found, been called away from his breakfast to a patient. Hewitt followed him in the direction of the patient's house, and met him returning. They walked together, and presently, as they came in sight of a row of houses, a girl, having the appearance of a maid-of-all-work, came running from the side door of the end house—a house rather larger and more pretentious than the others in the row. Almost immediately a policeman appeared from the front door, and, seeing the girl running, shouted to Hewitt and his companion to stop her. This Hewitt did by a firm though gentle grasp of the arms, and, turning her about, marched her back again. "Come, come," he said, "you'll gain nothing by running away, whatever it is." But the girl shuddered and sobbed, and cried incoherently, "No, no—don't; I'm afraid. I don't like it, sir. It's awful. I can't stop there."

She was a strongly-built, sullen-looking girl, with prominent eyebrows and a rather brutal expression of face, consequently her extreme nervous agitation, her distorted face and her tears were the more noticeable.

"What is all this?" the surgeon asked as they reached the front door of the house. "Girl in trouble?"

The policeman touched his helmet. "It's murder, sir, this time," he said, "that's what it is. I've sent for the inspector, and I've sent for you too, sir; and of course I couldn't allow anyone to leave the house till I'd handed it over to the inspector. Come," he added to the girl, as he saw her indoors, "don't let's have any more o' that. It looks bad, I can tell you."

"Where's the body?" asked the surgeon.

"First-floor front, sir—bed-sittin'-room. Ship's captain, I'm told. Throat cut awful."

"Come," said the surgeon, as he prepared to mount the stairs. "You'd better come up too, Mr. Hewitt. You may spot something that will help if it's a difficult case."

Together they entered the room, and indeed the sight was of a sort that any maidservant might be excused for running away from. Between the central table and the fireplace the body lay fully clothed, and the whole room was in a great state of confusion, drawers lying about with the contents spilt, boxes open, and papers scattered about. On a table was a bottle and a glass.

"Robbery, evidently," the surgeon said as he bent to his task. "See, the pockets are all emptied and partly protruding at the top. The watch and chain has been torn off, leaving the swivel in the button-hole."

"Yes," Hewitt answered, "that is so." He had taken a rapid glance about the room, and was now examining the stove, a register, with close attention. He shut the trap above it and pushed to the room door. Then very carefully, by the aid of the feather end of a quill pen which lay on the table, he shifted the charred remains of a piece or two of paper from the top of the cold cinders into the fire shovel. He carried them to the sideboard, nearer the light from the window, and examined them minutely, making a few notes in his pocket-book, and then, removing the glass shade from an ornament on the mantelpiece, placed it over them.

"There's something that may be of some use to the police," he remarked, "or may not, as the case may be. At any rate there it is, safe from draughts, if they want it. There's nothing distinguishable on one piece, but I think the other has been a cheque."

The surgeon had concluded his first rapid examination and rose to his feet. "A very deep cut," he said, "and done from behind, I think, as he was sitting in his chair. Death at once, without a doubt, and has been dead seven or eight hours I should say. Bed not slept in, you see. Couldn't have done it himself, that's certain."

"The knife," Hewitt added, "is either gone or hidden. But here is the inspector."

The inspector was a stranger to Hewitt, and looked at him inquiringly, till the surgeon introduced him and mentioned his profession. Then he said, with the air of one unwillingly relaxing a rule of conduct, "All right, doctor, if he's a friend of yours. A little practice for you, eh, Mr. Hewitt?"

"Yes," Hewitt answered modestly. "I haven't had the advantage of any experience in the police force, and perhaps I may learn. Perhaps also I may help you."

This did not seem to strike the inspector as a very luminous probability, and he stepped to the landing and ordered up the constable to make his full report. He had brought another man with him, who took charge of the door. By this time, thinly populated as was the neighbourhood, boys had begun to collect outside.

The policeman's story was simple. As he passed on his beat he had been called by three women who had a light ladder planted against the window-sill of the room. They feared something was wrong with the occupant of the room, they said, as they could not make him hear, and his door was locked, therefore they had brought the ladder to look in at the window, but now each feared to go and look. Would he, the policeman, do so? He mounted the ladder, looked in at the window, and saw—what was still visible.

He had then, at the women's urgent request, entered the house, broken in the door, and found the body to be dead and cold. He had told the women at once, and warned them, in the customary manner, that any statement they might be disposed to volunteer would be noted and used as evidence. The landlady, who was a widow, and gave her name as Mrs. Beckle, said that the dead man's name was Abel Pullin, and that he was a captain in the merchant service, who had occupied the room as a lodger since the end of last week only, when he had returned from a voyage. So far as she knew no stranger had been in the house since she last saw Pullin alive on the previous evening, and the only person living in the house, who had since gone out, was Mr. Foster, also a seafaring man, who had been a mate, but for some time had had no ship. He had gone out an hour or so before the discovery was made—earlier than usual, and without breakfast. That was all that Mrs. Beckle knew, and the only other persons in the house were the servant and a Miss Walker, a school teacher. They knew nothing; but Miss Walker was very anxious to be allowed to go to her school, which of course he had not allowed till the inspector should arrive.

"That's all right," the inspector said. "And you're sure the door was locked?"

"Yes, sir, fast."

"Key in the lock?"

"No, sir. I haven't seen any key."

"Window shut, just as it is now?"

"Yes, sir; nothing's been touched."

The inspector walked to the window and opened it. It was a wooden-framed casement window, fastened by the usual turning catch at the side, with a heavy bow handle. He just glanced out and then swung the window carelessly to on its hinges. The catch, however, worked so freely that the handle dropped and the catch banged against the window frame as he turned away. Hewitt saw this and closed the casement properly, after a glance at the sill.

The inspector made a rapid examination of the clothing on the body, and then said, "It's a singular thing about the key. The door was locked fast, but there's no key to be seen inside the room. Seems it must have been locked from the outside."

"Perhaps," Hewitt suggested, "other keys on this lauding tit the lock. It's commonly the case in this sort of house."

"That's so," the inspector admitted, with the air of encouraging a pupil. "We'll see."

They walked across the landing to the nearest door. It had a small round brass escutcheon, apparently recently placed there. "Yale lock;" said the inspector. "That's no good." They went to the third door, which stood ajar.

"Seems to be Mr. Foster's room," the inspector remarked; "here's the key inside."

They took it across the landing and tried it. It fitted Captain Pullin's lock exactly and easily. "Hullo!" said the inspector, "look at that!"

Hewitt nodded thoughtfully. Just then he became aware of somebody behind him, who had arrived noiselessly. He turned and saw a mincing little woman, with a pursed mouth and lofty expression, who took no notice of him but addressed the inspector. "I shall be glad to know, if you please," she said, "when I may leave the house and attend to my duties. My school has already been open for three-quarters of an hour, and I cannot conceive why I am detained in this manlier."

"Very sorry, ma'am," the inspector replied. "Matter of duty, of course. Perhaps we shall be able to let you go presently. Meanwhile perhaps you can help us. You're not obliged to say anything, of course, but if you do we shall make a note of it. You didn't hear any uncommon noise in the night, did you?"

"Nothing at all. I retired at ten and I was asleep soon after. I know nothing whatever of the whole horrible affair, and I shall leave the house entirely as soon as I can arrange."

"Did you have any opportunity of observing Mr. Pullin's manners or habits?" Hewitt asked.

"Indeed, no. I saw nothing of him. But I could hear him very often, and his language was not of the sort I could tolerate. He seemed to dominate the whole house with his boorish behaviour, and he was frequently intoxicated. I had already told Mrs. Beckle that if his stay were to continue mine should cease. I avoided him, indeed, altogether, and I know nothing of him."

"Do you know how he came here? Did he know Mrs. Beckle or anybody else in the house before?"

"That also I can't say. But Mrs. Beckle, I believe, knew all about him. In fact I have sometimes thought there was some mysterious connection between them, though what I cannot say. Certainly I cannot understand a landlady keeping so troublesome a lodger."

"You have seen a little more of Mr. Foster, of course?"

"Well, yes. He has been here so much longer. He was more endurable than was Captain Pullin, certainly, though he was not always sober. The two did not love one another, I believe."

There the inspector pricked his ears. "They didn't love one another, you say, ma'am. Why was that?"

"Oh, I don't really know. I fancy Mr. Foster wanted to borrow money or something. He used to say Captain Pullin had plenty of money, and had once sunk a ship purposely. I don't know whether or not this was serious, of course."

Hewitt looked at her keenly. "Have you ever heard him called Captain Pullin of the Egret?" he asked.

"No, I never heard the name of any vessel."

"There's just one thing, Miss Walker," the inspector said, "that I'm afraid I must insist on before you go. It's only a matter of form, of course. But I must ask you to let me look round your room—I shan't disturb it."

Miss Walker tossed her head. "Very well then," she said, turning toward the door with the Yale lock, and producing the key; "there it is." And she flung the door open.

The inspector stepped within and took a perfunctory glance round. "That will do; thank you," he said; "I am sorry to have kept you. I think you may go now, Miss Walker. You won't be leaving here to-day altogether, I suppose?"

"No, I'm afraid I can't. Good-morning."

As she disappeared by the foot of the stairs the inspector remarked in a jocular undertone, "Needn't bother about her. She isn't strong enough to cut a hen's throat."

Just then Miss Walker appeared again and attempted to take her umbrella from the stand—a heavy, tall oaken one. The ribs, however, had become jammed between the stand and the wall; so Miss Walker, with one hand, calmly lifted the stand and disengaged the umbrella with the other. "My eyes!" observed the inspector, "she's a bit stronger than she looks."

The surgeon came upon the landing. "I shall send to the mortuary now," he said.

"I've seen all I want to see here. Have you seen the landlady?"

"No. I think she's downstairs."

They went downstairs and found Mrs. Beckle in the back room, much agitated, though she was not the sort of woman one would expect to find greatly upset by anything. She was thin, hard and rigid, with the rigidity and sharpness that women acquire who have a long and lonely struggle with poverty. She had at first very little to say. Captain Pullin had lodged with her before. Last night he had been in all the evening and had gone to bed about half-past eleven, and by a quarter past everybody else had done so, and the house was fastened up for the night. The front door was fully bolted and barred, and it was found so in the morning. No stranger had been in the house for some days. The only person who had left before the discovery was Mr. Foster, and he went away when only the servant was up.

This was unusual, as he usually took breakfast in the house. What had frightened the girl so much, she thought, was the fact that after the door had been burst open she peeped into the room, out of curiosity, and was so horrified at the sight that she ran out of the house. She had always been a hardworking girl, though of sullen habits.

The inspector made more particular inquiries as to Mr. Foster, and after some little reluctance Mrs. Beckle gave her opinion that he was very short of money indeed. He had lost his ship sometime back through a neglect of duty, and he was not of altogether sober habits; he had consequently been unable to get another berth as yet. It was a fact, she admitted, that he owed her a considerable sum for rent, but he had enough clothes and nautical implements in his boxes to cover that and more.

Hewitt had been watching Mrs. Beckle's face very closely, and now suddenly asked, with pointed emphasis, "How long have you known Mr. Pullin?"

Mrs. Beckle faltered and returned Hewitt's steadfast gaze with a quick glance of suspicion. "Oh," she said, "I have known him, on and off, for a long time."

"A connection by marriage, of course?" Hewitt's hard gaze was still upon her.

Mrs. Beckle looked from him to the inspector and back again, and the corners of her mouth twitched. Then she sat down and rested her head on her hand. "Well, I suppose I must say it, though I've kept it to myself till now," she said resignedly. "He's my brother-in-law."

"Of course, as you have been told, you are not obliged to say anything now; but the more information you can give the better chance there may be of detecting your brother-in-law's murderer."

"Well, I don't mind, I'm sure. It was a bad day when he married my sister. He killed her—not at once, so that he might have been hung for it, but by a course of regular brutality and starvation. I hated the man!" she said, with a quick access of passion, which however she suppressed at once.

"And yet you let him stay in your house?"

"Oh, I don't know. I was afraid of him; and he used to come just when he pleased, and practically take possession of the house. I couldn't keep him away; and he drove away my other lodgers." She suddenly fired up again. "Wasn't that enough to make anybody desperate? Can you wonder at anything?"

She quieted again by a quick effort, and Hewitt and the inspector exchanged glances.

"Let me see, he was captain of the sailing ship Egret, wasn't he?" Hewitt asked. "Lost in the Pacific a year or more ago?"

"Yes."

"If I remember the story of the loss aright, he and one native hand—a Kanaka boy—were the only survivors?"

"Yes, they were the only two. He was the only one that came back to England."

"Just so. And there were rumours, I believe, that after all he wasn't altogether a loser by that wreck? Mind, I only say there were rumours; there may have been nothing in them."

"Yes," Mrs. Beckle replied, "I know all about that. They said the ship had been east away purposely, for the sake of the insurance. But there was no truth in that, else why did the underwriters pay? And besides, from what I know privately, it couldn't have been. Abel Pullin was a reckless scoundrel enough, I know, but he would have taken good care to be paid well for any villainy of that sort."

"Yes, of course. But it was suggested that he was."

"No, nothing of the sort. He came here, as usual, as soon as he got home, and until he got another ship he hadn't a penny. I had to keep him, so I know. And he was sober almost all the time from want of money. Do you mean to say, if the common talk were true, that he would have remained like that without getting money of the owners, his accomplices, and at least making them give him another ship? Not he. I know him too well."

"Yes, no doubt. He was now just back from his next voyage after that, I take it?"

"Yes, in the Iolanthe brig. A smaller ship than he has been used to, and belonging to different owners."

"Had he much money this time?"

"No. He had bought himself a gold watch and chain abroad, and he had a ring and a few pounds in money, and sonic instruments, that was all, I think, in addition to his clothes."

"Well, they've all been stolen now," the inspector said. "Have you missed anything yourself?"

"No."

"Nor the other lodgers, so far as you know?"

"No, neither of them."

"Very well, Mrs. Beckle. We'll have a word or two with the servant now, and then I'll get you to come over the house with us."

Sarah Taffs was the servant's name. She seemed to have got over her agitation, and was now sullen and uncommunicative. She would say nothing. "You said I needn't say nothin' if I didn't want to, and I won't." That was all she would say, and she repeated it again and again. Once, however, in reply to a question as to Foster, she flashed out angrily, "If it's Mr. Foster you're after you won't find 'im. 'E's a gentleman, 'e is, and I ain't goin' to tell you nothin'." But that was all.

Then Mrs. Beckle showed the inspector, the surgeon and Hewitt over the house. Everything was in perfect order on the ground floor and on the stairs. The stairs, it appeared, had been swept before the discovery was made. Nevertheless Hewitt and the inspector scrutinised them narrowly. The top floor consisted of two small rooms only, used as bedrooms by Mrs. Beckle and Sarah Taffs respectively. Nothing was missing, and everything was in order there.

The one floor between contained the dead man's room, Miss Walker's and Foster's. Miss Walker's room they had already seen, and now they turned into Foster's.

The place seemed to betray careless habits on the part of its tenant, and was everywhere in slovenly confusion. The bed-clothes were flung anyhow on the floor, and a chair was overturned. Hewitt looked round the room and remarked that there seemed to be no clothes hanging about, as might have been expected.

II

"No," Mrs. Beckle replied; "he has taken to keeping them all in his boxes lately."

"How many boxes has he?" asked the inspector.

"Only these two?"

"That is all."

The inspector stooped and tried the lids.

"Both locked," he said. "I think we'll take the liberty of a peep into these boxes."

He produced a bunch of keys and tried them all, but none fitted. Then Hewitt felt about inside the locks very carefully with a match, and then taking a button-hook from his pocket, after a little careful "humouring" work, turned both the locks, one after another, and lifted the lids.

Mrs. Beckle uttered an exclamation of dismay, and the inspector looked at her rather quizzically. The boxes contained nothing but bricks.

"Ah," said the inspector, "I've seen that sort of suits o' clothes before. People have 'em who don't pay hotel bills and such-like. You're a very good pick-lock, by the way, Mr. Hewitt. I never saw anything quicker and neater."

"But I know he had a lot of clothes," Mrs. Beckle protested. "I've seen them."

"Very likely—very likely indeed," the inspector answered. "But they're gone now, and Mr. Foster's gone with 'em."

"But—but the girl didn't say he had any bundles with him when he went out?"

"No, she didn't; and she didn't say he hadn't, did she? She won't say anything about him, and she says she won't, plump. Even supposing he hadn't got them with him this morning that signifies nothing. The clothes are gone, and anybody intending a job of that sort"—the inspector jerked his thumb significantly towards the skipper's room—"would get his things away quietly first so as to have no difficulty about getting away himself afterwards. No; the thing's pretty plain now, I think; and I'm afraid Mr. Foster's a pretty bad lot. Anyway I shouldn't like to be in his shoes."

"Nor I," Hewitt assented. "Evidence of that sort isn't easy to get over."

"Come, Mrs. Beckle," the inspector said, "do you mind coming into the front room with us? The body's covered over with a rug."

The landlady disliked going, it was plain to see, but presently she pulled herself together and followed the men. She peeped once distrustfully round the door to where the body lay and then resolutely turned her back on it.

"His watch and chain are gone and whatever else he had in his pockets," the inspector said. "I think you said he had a ring?"

"Yes, one—a thick gold one."

"Then that's gone too. Everything's turned upside down, and probably other things are stolen too. Do you miss any?"

"Yes," Mrs. Beckle replied, looking round, but avoiding with her eyes the rug-covered heap near the fireplace. "There was a sextant on the mantelpiece; it was his; and he kept one or two other instruments in that drawer "—pointing to one which had been turned out—"but they seem to be gone now. And there was a small ship, carved in ivory, and worth money, I believe—that's gone. I don't know about his clothes; some of them may be stolen or they may not." She stepped to the bed and turned back the coverlet. "Oh," she added, "the sheets are gone from the bed too!"

"Usual thing," the inspector remarked; "wrap up the swag in a sheet, you know—makes a convenient bundle. Nothing else missing?"

The landlady took one more look round and said doubtfully, "No, no, I don't think so. Oh, but yes," she suddenly added, "uncle's hook."

"Oh," remarked the inspector with dismal jocularity, "he's took uncle's hook as well as his own, has he? What was uncle's hook like?"

"It wasn't of much value," Mrs. Beckle explained; "but I kept it as a memorial. My great uncle, who died many years ago, was a sea-captain too, and had lost his left hand by accident. He wore a hook in its place—a hook made for him on board his vessel. It was an iron hook screwed into a wooden stock. He had it taken off in his last illness and gave it to me to mind against his recovery. But he never got well, so I've kept it over since. It used to hang on a nail at the side of the chimney-breast."

"No wounds about the body that might have been made with a hook like that, doctor, were there?" the inspector asked.

"No, no wounds at all but the one."

"Well, well," the inspector said, moving toward the door, "we've got to find Foster now, that's plain. I'll see about it. You've sent to the mortuary you say, doctor? All right. You've no particular reason for sending the girl out of doors to-day, I suppose, Mrs. Beckle?"

"I can keep her in, of course," the landlady answered. "It will be inconvenient, though."

"Ah, then keep her in, will you? We mustn't lose sight of her. I'll leave a couple of men here, of course, and I'll tell them she mustn't be allowed out."

Hewitt and the surgeon went downstairs and parted at the door. "I shall be over again to-morrow morning," Hewitt said, "about that other matter I was speaking of. Shall I find you in?"

"Well," the doctor answered, "at any rate they will tell you where I am. Good morning."

"Good morning," Hewitt answered, and then stopped. "I'm obliged for being allowed to look about upstairs here," he said. "I'm not sure what the inspector has in his mind, by the way; but I should think whatever I noticed would be pretty plain to him, though naturally he would be cautious about talking of it before others, as I was myself. That being the case it might seem rather presumptuous in me to make suggestions, especially as he seems fairly confident. But if you have a chance presently of giving him a quiet hint you might draw his special attention to two things—the charred paper that I took from the fireplace and the missing hook. There is a good deal in that, I fancy. I shall have an hour or two to myself, I expect, this afternoon, and I'll make a small inquiry or two on my own account in town. If anything comes of them I'll let you know to-morrow when I see you."

"Very well, I shall expect you. Goodbye."

Hewitt did not go straight away from the house to the railway station. He took a turn or two about the row of houses, and looked up each of the paths leading from them across the surrounding marshy fields. Then he took the path for the station. About a hundred yards along, the path reached a deep muddy ditch with a high hedge behind it, and then lay by the side of the ditch for some little distance before crossing it. Hewitt stopped and looked thoughtfully at the ditch for a few moments before proceeding, and then went briskly on his way.

That evening's papers were all agog with the mysterious murder of a ship's captain at West Ham, and in next morning's papers it was announced that Henry Foster, a seafaring man, and lately mate of a trading ship, had been arrested in connection with the crime.

II

That morning Hewitt was at the surgeon's house early. The surgeon was in, and saw him at once. His own immediate business being transacted, Hewitt learned particulars of the arrest of Foster. "The man actually came back of his own accord in the afternoon," the surgeon said. "Certainly he was drunk, but that seems a very reckless sort of thing, even for a drunken man. One rather curious thing was that he asked for Pullin as soon as he arrived, and insisted on going to him to borrow half-a-sovereign. Of course he was taken into custody at once, and charged, and that seemed to sober him very quickly. He seemed dazed for a bit, and then, when he realised the position he was in, refused to say a word. I saw him at the station. He had certainly been drinking a good deal; but a curious thing was that he hadn't a cent of money on him. He'd soon got rid of it all, anyhow."

"Did you say anything to the inspector as to the things I mentioned to you?"

"Yes, but he didn't seem to think a great deal of them. He took a look at the charred paper and saw that one piece had evidently been a cheque on the Eastern Consolidated Bank, but the other he couldn't see any sort of sign upon. As to the hook, he seemed to take it that that was used to fasten in the knot of the bundle, to carry it the more easily."

"Well," Hewitt said, "I think I told you yesterday that I should make an inquiry or two myself? Yes, I did. I've made those inquiries, and now I think I can give the inspector some help. What is his name, by the way?"

"Truscott. He's a very good sort of fellow, really."

"Very well. Shall I find him at the station?"

"Probably, unless he's off duty; that I don't know about. But I should call at the house first, I think, if I were you. That is much nearer than the station, and he might possibly be there. Even if he isn't, there will be a constable, and he can tell you where to find Truscott."

Hewitt accordingly made for the house, and had the good fortune to overtake Truscott on his way there. "Good morning, inspector," he called cheerily. "I've got some information for you, I think."

"Oh, good morning. What is it?"

"It's in regard to that business," Hewitt replied, indicating by a nod the row of houses a hundred yards ahead. "But it will be clearer if we go over the whole thing together and take what I have found out in its proper place. You're not altogether satisfied with your capture of Foster, are you?"

"Well, I mustn't say, of course. Perhaps not. We've traced his doings yesterday after he left the house, and perhaps it doesn't help us much. But what do you know?"

"I'll tell you. But first can you get hold of such a thing as a boat-hook? Any long pole with a hook on the end will do."

"I don't know that there's one handy. Perhaps they'll have a garden rake at the house, if that'll do?"

"Excellently, I should thick, if it's fairly long. We will ask."

The garden rake was forthcoming at once, and with it Hewitt and the inspector made their way along the path that led towards the railway station and stopped where it came by the ditch.

"I've brought you here purely on a matter of conjecture," Hewitt said, "and there may be nothing in it; but if there is it will help us. This is a very muddy ditch, with a soft bottom many feet deep probably, judging from the wet nature of the soil hereabout."

He took the rake and plunged it deep into the ditch, dragging it slowly back up the side. It brought up a tangle of duckweed and rushes and slimy mud, with a stick or two among it.

"Do you think the knife's been thrown here?" asked the inspector.

"Possibly, and possibly something else. We'll see." And Hewitt made another dive. They went along thus very thoroughly and laboriously, dragging every part of the ditch as they went, it being frequently necessary for both to pull together to get the rake through the tangle of weed and rubbish. They had worked through seven or eight yards from the angle of the path where it approached the ditch, when Hewitt stopped, with the rake at the bottom.

"Here is something that feels a little different," he said. "I'll get as good a hold as I can and then we'll drag it up slowly and steadily together."

He gave the rake a slight twist and then the two pulled steadily. Presently the sunken object came away suddenly, as though mud-suction had kept it under, and rose easily to the surface. It was a muddy mass, and they had to swill it to and fro a few times in the clearer upper water before it was seen to be a linen bundle. They drew it ashore and untied the thick knot at the top. Inside was an Indian shawl, also knotted, and this they opened also. There within, wet and dirty, lay a sextant, a chronometer in a case, a gold watch and chain, a handful of coins, a thick gold ring, a ship carved in ivory, with much of the delicate work broken, a sealskin waistcoat, a door key, a seamen's knife, and an iron hook screwed into a wooden stock.

"Lord!" exclaimed Inspector Truscott, "what's this? It's a queer place to hide swag of this sort. Why, that watch and those instruments must be ruined."

"Yes, I'm afraid so," Hewitt answered. "You see the things are wrapped in the sheets, just as you expected. But those sheets mean something more. There are two, you notice."

"Yes, of course; but I don't see what it points to. The whole thing's most odd. Foster certainly would have been a fool to hide the things here; he's a sailor himself, and knows better than to put away chronometers and sextants in a wet ditch—unless he got frightened, and put the things there out of sight because the murder was discovered."

"But you say you have traced his movements after he left. If he had come near here while the police were about he would have been seen from the house. No, you've got the wrong prisoner. The person who put those things there didn't want them again."

"Then do you think robbery wasn't the motive after all?"

"Yes, it was; but not this robbery. Conic, we'll talk it over in the house, Let us take these things with us."

Arrived at the house Hewitt immediately locked, bolted and barred the front door.

Then he very carefully and gently unfastened each lock, bolt and bar in order, pressing the door with his hand and taking every precaution to avoid noise. Nevertheless the noise was considerable. There was a sad lack of oil everywhere, and all the bolts creaked; the lock in particular made a deal of noise, and when the key was half turned its bolt shot back with a loud thump.

"Anybody who had once heard that door fastened or unfastened," said Hewitt, "would hesitate about opening it in the dead of night after committing murder. He would remember the noise. Do you mind taking the things up to the room—the room—upstairs? I will go and ask Mrs Beckle a question."

Truscott went upstairs, and presently

Hewitt followed. "I have just asked Mrs. Beckle," he said, "whether or not the captain went to the front door for any purpose on the evening before his death. She says he stood there for some half an hour or so smoking his pipe before he went to bed. We shall see what that means presently, I. think. Now we will go into the thing in the light of what I have found out."

"Yes, tell me that."

"Very well. I think it will make the thing plainer if I summarise separately all my conclusions from the evidence as a whole from the beginning. Perhaps the same ideas struck you, but I'm sure you'll excuse my going over them. Now here was a man undoubtedly murdered, and the murderer was gone from the room. There were two ways by which he could have gone the door and the window. If he went by the window, then he was somebody who did not live in the place, since nobody seemed to have been missing when the girl came down, though, mind you, it was necessary to avoid relying on all she said, in view of her manner, and her almost acknowledged determination not to incriminate Foster. It seemed at first sight probable that the murderer had gone out by the door, because the key was gone entirely, and if he had left by the window he would probably have left the key in the lock to hinder anybody who attempted to get in with another key, or to peep. But then the blind was up, and was found so in the morning. It would probably be pulled down at dark, and the murderer would be unlikely to raise it except to go out that way. But then the casement was shut and fastened. Just so; but can't it be as easily shut and fastened from the outside as from the in? The catch is very loose, and swings by itself. True, this prevents the casement shutting when it is just carelessly banged to, but see here." He rose and went to the window. "Anybody from outside who cared to hold the catch back with his finger till the casement was shut as far as the frame could then shut the window completely, and the catch would simply swing into its appointed groove.

"And now see something more. You and I both looked at the sill outside. It is a smooth new sill—the house itself is almost new; but probably you saw in one place a sharply marked pit or depression. Look, it seems to have been drilled with a sharp steel point. It was absolutely new, for there was the powder of the stone about the mark. The wind has since blown the powder away. Now if a man had descended from that sill by means of a rope with a hook at the end that was just the sort of mark I should expect him to leave behind. So that at any rate the balance of probability was that the murderer had left by the window. But there is another thing which confirms this. You will remember that when Mrs. Beckle mentioned that the sheets were gone from the bed you concluded that they had been taken to carry the swag."

"Yes, and so they were, as we have seen here in the bundle."

"Just so; but why both sheets? One would be ample. And since you allude to the bundle, why both sheets as well as the Indian shawl? This last, by the way, is a thing Mrs. Beckle seems not to have missed in the confusion, or perhaps she didn't know that Pullin possessed it. Why all these wrappings, and moreover, why the hook? The presumption is clear. The bundle was already made up in the Indian shawl and required no more wrapping. The two sheets were wanted to tie together to enable the criminal to descend from the window, and the hook was the very thing to hold this rope with at the top. It was not necessary to tie it to anything, and it would not prevent the shutting of the window behind. Moreover, when the descent had been made, a mere shake of the rope of sheets would dislodge the hook and bring it down, thus leaving no evidence of the escape—except the mark on the sill, which was very small.

"Then again, there was no noise or struggle heard. Pullin, as you could see, was a powerful, hard-set man, not likely to allow his throat to be cut without a lot of trouble, therefore the murderer must either have entered the room unknown to him—an unlikely thing, for he had not gone to bed—or else must have been there with his permission, and must have taken him by sudden surprise. And now we come to the heart of the thing. Of the two papers burnt in the grate—you have kept them under the shade I see—one bore no trace of the writing that had been on it (many inks and papers do not after having been burnt), but the other bore plain signs of having been a cheque. Now just let us look at it. The main body of the paper has burnt to a deep gray ash, nearly black, but the printed parts of the cheque—those printed in coloured inks, that is—are of a much paler gray, quite a light ash colour. That is the colour to which most of the pink ink used in printing cheques burns, as you may easily test for yourself with an old cheque of the sort that is printed from a fine plate with water-solution pink ink. The black ink, on the other hand, such as the number of the cheque is printed in, has charred black, and by sharp eyes is quite distinguishable against the general dark gray of the paper. The cinder is unfortunately broken rather badly, and the part containing the signature is missing altogether. But one can plainly see in large script letters part of the boldest line of print, the name of the bank. The letters are e r n C o n s o, and this must mean the Eastern Consolidated Bank. Of course you saw that for yourself."

"Yes, of course I did."

"Fortunately the whole of the cheque number is unbroken. It is Of course I took a note of that, as well as of the other particulars distinguishable. It is payable to Pullin, clearly, for here is the latter half of his Christian name, Abel, and the first few letters of Pullin. Then on the line where the amount is written at length there are the letters u s a n d and p. Plainly it was a large cheque, for thousands. At the bottom, where the amount is placed in figures, there is a bad break, but the first figure is a 2. The cheque, then, was one for £2000 at least. And there is one more thing. The cinder is perfect and unbroken nearly all along the top edge, and there is no sign of crossing, so that here is an open cheque which any thief might cash with a little care. That is all we can see, but it is enough, I think. Now would a thief, committing murder for the sake of plunder, burn this cheque? Would Pullin, to whom the money was to be paid, burn it? I think not. Then who in the whole world would have any interest in burning it? Not a soul, with one single exception—the man who drew it."

"Yes, yes. What! do you mean that the man who drew that cheque must have murdered Pullin in order to get it back and destroy it?"

"That is my opinion. Now who would draw Pullin a cheque for £2000? Anybody in this house? Is it at all likely? Of course not. Again, we are pointed to a stranger. And now remember Pullin's antecedents. On his last voyage but one his ship the Egret, from Valparaiso for Wellington, New Zealand, was cast away on the Paumotu Islands, far out of her proper course. There was but a small crew, and, as it happened, all were lost except Pullin and one Kanaka boy. The Egret was heavily insured, and there were nasty rumours at Lloyd's that Captain Pullin had made sure of his whereabouts, taken care of himself, and destroyed the ship in collusion with the owners, and that the Kanaka boy had only escaped because he happened to be well acquainted with the islands. But there was nothing positive in the way of proof, and the underwriters paid, with no more than covert grumblings. And, as you remember, Mrs. Heckle told us yesterday Pullin on his return had no money. Now suppose the story of the intentional wreck were true, and for some reason Pullin's payment was put off till after his next voyage. Would the people who sent their men to death in the Pacific hesitate at a single murder to save £2000? I think not.

"After I left you yesterday I made some particular inquiries at Lloyd's through a friend of mine, an underwriter himself. I find that the sole owner of the Egret was one Herbert Roofe, trading as Herbert Roofe & Co. The firm is a very small one, as shipping concerns go, and has had the reputation for a long time of being very 'rocky' financially; indeed it was the common talk at Lloyd's that nothing but the wreck of the Egret saved Roofe from the Bankruptcy Court, and he is supposed now to be 'hanging on by his eyelashes,' as my friend expresses it, with very little margin to keep him going, and in a continual state of touch-and-go between his debit and credit sides. As to the rumours of the wilful casting away of the Egret, my friend assured me that the thing was as certain as anything could be, short of legal proof. There was something tricky about the cargo, and altogether it was a black sort of business. And to complete things he told me that the bankers of Herbert Roofe & Co. were the Eastern Consolidated."

"Phew! This is getting pretty warm, I must say, Mr. Hewitt."

"Wait a minute; my friend aided me a little further still. I told him the whole story—in confidence, of course—and he agreed to help. At my suggestion he went to the manager of the Eastern Consolidated Bank, whom he knew personally, and represented that among a heap of cheques one had got torn, and the missing piece destroyed. This was true entirely, except in regard to the heap—a little fiction which I trust my friend may be forgiven. The cheque, he said, was on the Eastern Consolidated, and its number was B/K63777. Would the manager mind telling him which of his customers had the cheque book from which that had been taken? Trace of where the cheque had come from had been quite lost, and it would save a lot of trouble if the Bank could let him know. 'Certainly,' said the manager; 'I'll inquire.' He did, and presently a clerk entered the room with the information that cheque No. B/K63777 was from a book in the possession of Messrs. Herbert Roofe & Co."

The inspector rose excitedly from his chair. "Come," he said, "this must be followed up. We mustn't waste time; there's no knowing where Roofe may have got to by this."

"Just a little more patience," Hewitt said. "I don't think there will be much difficulty in finding him. He believes himself safe. As soon as my friend told me what the Bank manager had said I went round to Roofe's office to ascertain his whereabouts, prepared with an excuse for the interview in case I should find him in. It was a small office, rather, over a shop in Leadenhall Street. When I asked for Mr. Roofe the clerk informed me that he was at home confined to his room by a bad cold, and had not been at the office since Tuesday—the next day but one before the body was discovered. I appeared to be disappointed, and asked if I could send him a message. Yes, I could, the clerk told me. All letters were being sent to him, and he was sending business instructions daily to the office from Chadwell Heath. I saw that the address had slipped inadvertently from the clerk's mouth, for it is a general rule, I know, in city offices, to keep the principals' addresses from casual callers. So I said no more, but contented myself with the information I had got. I took the first opportunity of looking at a suburban directory, and then I found the name of Mr. Roofe's house at Chadwell Heath. It is Scarby Lodge."

"I must be off, then, at once," Truscott said, "and make careful inquiries as to his movements. And those cinders—bless my soul, they're as precious as diamonds now! How shall we keep them from damage?"

"Oh, the glass shade will do, I fancy. But wait a moment; let us review things thoroughly. I will run rapidly over what I suggest has happened between Roofe and Pullin, and you shall stop me if you see any flaw in the argument. It's best to make our impressions clear and definite. Now we will suppose that the Egret has been lost, and Pullin has come home to claim the reward of his infamy. We will suppose it is £2000. He goes to Roofe and demands it. Roofe says he can't possibly pay just then; he is very hard up, and the insurance money of the Egret has only just saved him from bankruptcy. Pullin insists on having his money. But, says Roofe, that is impossible, because he hasn't got it. A cheque for the amount would be dishonoured. The plunder of the underwriters has all been used to keep things going. Roofe says plainly that Pullin must wait for the money. Pullin can't reveal the conspiracy without implicating himself, and Roofe knows it. He promises to pay in a certain time, and gives Pullin an acknowledgment of the debt, an IOU, perhaps, or something of that kind, and with that Pullin has to be contented, and, having no money, he has to go away on another voyage, this time in a ship belonging to somebody else, became it would look worse than ever if Roofe gave him another berth at once. He makes his voyage and he returns, and asks for his money again. But Roofe is as bard up as ever. He cannot pay, and he cannot refuse to pay. It is ruin either way. He knows that Pullin will stand no more delay, and may do something desperate, so Roofe does something desperate himself. He tells Pullin that he must not call at his office, nor must anybody see them together anywhere for fear of suspicion. He suggests that he, Roofe, should call at Pullin's lodgings late one night, and bring the money. Pullin is to let him in himself, so that nobody may see him. Pullin consents, and thus assists in the concealment of his own murder. He waits at the front door smoking his pipe (you remember that Mrs. Beckle told me so), waiting for Roofe. When Roofe comes Pullin takes him very quietly up to his room without attracting attention. Roofe, on his part, has prepared things by feigning a bad cold and going to bed early, going out—perhaps through the window—when all his household is quiet. There are plenty of late trains from Chadwell Heath that would bring him to Stratford.

"Well, when they are safely in Pullin's room Roofe hears the front door shut and bolted, with all its squeaks and thumps, and decides that it won't be safe to go out that way after he has committed his crime. The men sit and talk, and Pullin drinks. Roofe doesn't. You will remember the bottle on the table, with only one glass. Roofe produces and writes a cheque for the £2000, and Pullin hands back the IOU, which Roofe burns. That would be the lower of the two charred pieces of paper, which we have there with the other, but can't read.

"Then the crime takes place. Perhaps Pullin drinks a little too much. At any rate Roofe gets behind him, uses the sharp seaman's knife he has brought for the purpose, and straightway the skipper is dead at his feet. Then Roofe gets back the cheque and burns that. After that he ransacks the whole room. He fears there may be some documentary evidence, which, being examined, may throw some light on the Egret affair. Then he sets about his escape. To make the thing look like a murder for ordinary plunder, and at the same time account for the upset room, he takes away all the dead man's valuables tied in that shawl. He sees the hook—just the thing he wants—and of course the sheets are an obvious substitute for a rope. He takes away the door-key, to make it seem likely that somebody inside the house had been the criminal, and then he simply goes away through the window, as I have already explained. At 5.45 there would be a train to Chadwell Heath, and that would land him home early enough to enable him to regain his bedroom unobserved. After that he wisely maintains the pretence of illness for a day or two.

"I guessed that the things carried off would be in that ditch, for very simple reasons. I looked about the house, and the ditch seemed the only available hiding-place near. More, it was on the way to the station, the direction Roof e would naturally take. He would seize the very first opportunity of getting rid of his burden, for every possible reason. It was a nuisance to carry; he could not account for it if he were asked; and the further he carried it before getting rid of it the more distinct the clue to the direction he had taken, supposing it ever were found. The behaviour of some of the people in the house might have been suspicious, if I hadn't had so strong a clue in my hand, leading in another direction. Foster probably pawned all his clothes, and put those bricks in his boxes to conceal the fact, so that Mrs. Beckle might not turn him away. He owed her so much that at last he hadn't the face to go and eat her breakfast when he had no money to pay for it. He went out early, met friends, got 'stood' drinks and came back drunk. Probably he had been kind to the girl Taffs at some time or another, so that when she found he was suspected she refused to give any information."

"Yes," the inspector said, "it certainly seems to fit together. There's a future before you, Mr. Hewitt. But now I must go to Chadwell Heath. Are you coming?"

At Chadwell Heath it was found that a first-class return ticket to Stratford had been taken just before the 10.54 train left on the last night Abel Pullin was seen alive, and that the return half had been given up by a passenger who arrived by the first train soon after six in the morning The porter who took the ticket remembered the circumstance, because first-class tickets were rare at that time in the morning, but he did not recognise the passenger, who was muffled up.

"But I think there's enough for an arrest without a warrant, at any rate," Truscott said. "I am off to Scarby Lodge. Can't afford to waste any more time."

Scarby Lodge was a rather pretentious house. It was arranged that Truscott should wait aside till Hewitt had sent in a message asking to see Mr. Roofe on a matter of urgent business, and that then both should follow the servant to his room. This was done, and as the parlour maid was knocking at the bedroom door she was astonished to find Hewitt and the police inspector behind her. Truscott at once pushed open the door and the two walked in.

It was a large room, and at the end a man sat in his dressing-gown near a table on which stood several medicine bottles. He frowned as Truscott and Hewitt entered, but betrayed no sign of emotion, carelessly taking one of the small bottles from the table. "What do you want here?" he said.

"Sorry to be so unceremonious," Truscott said, "but I am a police officer, and it is my duty to arrest you on a serious charge of murder on the person of — Stop, sir! Let me see that!"

But it was too late. Before Truscott could reach him Roofe had swallowed the contents of the small bottle and, swaying once, dropped to the floor as though shot.

Hewitt stooped over the man. "Dead," he said, "dead as Abel Pullin. It is prussic acid. He had arranged for instant action if by any chance the game went against him."

But Inspector Truscott was troubled. "This is a nice thing," he said, "to have a prisoner commit suicide in front of my eyes. But you can testify that I hadn't time to get near him, can't you? Indeed he wasn't a prisoner at the time, for I hadn't arrested him, in fact."

IV. — THE CASE OF THE "FLITTERBAT LANCERS"

It was late on a summer evening, two or three years back, that I drowsed in my armchair over a particularly solid and ponderous volume of essays on social economy. I was doing a good deal of reviewing at the time, and I remember that this particular volume had a property of such exceeding toughness that I had already made three successive attacks on it, on as many successive evenings, each attack having been defeated in the end by sleep. The weather was hot, my chair was very comfortable, and the book had somewhere about its strings of polysyllables an essence as of laudanum. Still something had been done on each evening, and now on the fourth I strenuously endeavoured to finish the book. I was just beginning to feel that the words before me were sliding about and losing their meanings, when a sudden crash and a jingle of broken glass behind me woke me with a start, and I threw the book down. A pane of glass in my window was smashed, and I hurried across and threw up the sash to see, if I could, whence the damage had come.

The building in which my chambers (and Martin Hewitt's office) were situated was accessible—or rather visible, for there was no entrance—from the rear. There was, in fact, a small courtyard, reached by a passage from the street behind, and into this courtyard, my sitting-room window looked.

"Hullo, there!" I shouted. But there came no reply. Nor could I distinguish anybody in the courtyard. Some men had been at work during the day on a drainpipe, and I reflected that probably their litter had provided the stone with which my window had been smashed. As I looked, however, two men came hurrying from the passage into the court, and going straight into the deep shadow of one corner, presently appeared again in a less obscure part, hauling forth a third man, who must have already been there in hiding. The third man struggled fiercely, but without avail, and was dragged across toward the passage leading to the street beyond. But the most remarkable feature of the whole thing was the silence of all three men. No cry, no exclamation, escaped any of them. In perfect silence the two hauled the third across the courtyard, and in perfect silence he swung and struggled to resist and escape. The matter astonished me not a little, and the men were entering the passage before I found voice to shout at them. But they took no notice, and disappeared. Soon after I heard cab wheels in the street beyond, and had no doubt that the two men had carried off their prisoner.

I turned back into my room a little perplexed. It seemed probable that the man who had been borne off had broken my window. But why? I looked about on the floor, and presently found the missile. It was, as

I had expected, a piece of broken concrete, but it was wrapped up in a worn piece of paper, which had partly opened out as it lay on my carpet, thus indicating that it had just been crumpled round the stone.

I disengaged the paper and spread it out. Then I saw it to be a rather hastily written piece of manuscript music, whereof I append a reduced facsimile:

This gave me no help. I turned the paper this way and that, but could make nothing of it. There was not a mark on it that I could discover, except the music and the scrawled title, "Flitterbat Lancers," at the top.

The paper was old, dirty, and cracked. What did it all mean? One might conceive of a person in certain circumstances sending a message—possibly an appeal for help—through a friend's window, wrapped round a stone, but this seemed to be nothing of that sort.

Once more I picked up the paper, and with an idea to hear what the Flitterbat Lancers sounded like, I turned to my little pianette and strummed over the notes, making my own time and changing it as seemed likely. But I could by no means extract from the notes anything resembling an air. I half thought of trying Martin Hewitt's office door, in case he might still be there and offer a guess at the meaning of my smashed window and the scrap of paper, when Hewitt himself came in. He had stayed late to examine a bundle of papers in connection with a case just placed in his hands, and now, having finished, came to find if I were disposed for an evening stroll before turning in. I handed him the paper and the piece of concrete, observing, "There's a little job for you, Hewitt, instead of the stroll." And I told him the complete history of my smashed window.

Hewitt listened attentively, and examined both the paper and the fragment of paving. "You say these people made absolutely no sound whatever?" he asked.

"None but that of scuffling, and even that they seemed to do quietly."

"Could you see whether or not the two men gagged the other, or placed their hands over his mouth?"

"No, they certainly didn't do that. It was dark, of course, but not so dark as to prevent my seeing generally what they were doing."

Hewitt stood for half a minute in thought, and then said, "There's something in this, Brett—what, I can't guess at the moment, but something deep, I fancy. Are you sure you won't come out now?"

I told Hewitt that I was sure, and that I should stick to my work.

"Very well," he said; "then perhaps you will lend me these articles?" holding up the paper and the stone.

"Delighted," I said. "If you get no more melody out of the clinker than I did out of the paper, you won't have a musical evening. Goodnight!"

Hewitt went away with the puzzle in his hand, and I turned once more to my social economy, and, thanks to the gentleman who smashed my window, conquered.

At this time my only regular daily work was on an evening paper so that I left home at a quarter to eight on the morning following the adventure of my broken window, in order, as usual, to be at the office at eight; consequently it was not until lunchtime that I had an opportunity of seeing Hewitt. I went to my own rooms first, however, and on the landing by my door I found the housekeeper in conversation with a shortish, sun-browned man, whose accent at once convinced me that he hailed from across the Atlantic. He had called, it appeared, three or four times during the morning to see me, getting more impatient each time. As he did not seem even to know my name, the housekeeper had not considered it expedient to give him any information about me, and he was growing irascible under the treatment. When I at last appeared, however, he left her and approached me eagerly.

"See here, sir," he said, "I've been stumpin' these here durn stairs o' yours half through the mornin'. I'm anxious to apologize, and fix up some damage."

He had followed me into my sitting-room, and was now standing with his back to the fireplace, a dripping umbrella in one hand, and the forefinger of the other held up boulder-high and pointing, in the manner of a pistol, to my window, which, by the way, had been mended during the morning, in accordance with my instructions to the housekeeper.

"Sir," he continued, "last night I took the extreme liberty of smashin' your winder."

"Oh," I said, "that was you, was it?"

"It was, sir—me. For that I hev come humbly to apologize. I trust the draft has not discommoded you, sir. I regret the accident, and I wish to pay for the fixin' up and the general inconvenience." He placed a sovereign on the table. "I 'low you'll call that square now, sir, and fix things friendly and comfortable as between gentlemen, an' no ill will. Shake."

And he formally extended his hand.

I took it at once. "Certainly," I said. "As a matter of fact, you haven't inconvenienced me at all; indeed, there were some circumstances about the affair that rather interested me." And I pushed the sovereign toward him.

"Say now," he said, looking a trifle disappointed at my unwillingness to accept his money, "didn't I startle your nerves?"

"Not a bit," I answered, laughing. "In fact, you did me a service by preventing me going to sleep just when I shouldn't; so we'll say no more of that."

"Well—there was one other little thing," he pursued, looking at me rather sharply as he pocketed the sovereign. "There was a bit o' paper round that pebble that came in here. Didn't happen to notice that, did you?"

"Yes, I did. It was an old piece of manuscript music."

"That was it—exactly. Might you happen to have it handy now?"

"Well," I said, "as a matter of fact a friend of mine has it now. I tried playing it over once or twice, as a matter of curiosity, but I couldn't make anything of it, and so I handed it to him."

"Ah!" said my visitor, watching me narrowly, "that's a puzzler, that Flitterbat Lancers—a real puzzler. It whips 'em all. Ha, ha'." He laughed suddenly—a laugh that seemed a little artificial. "There's music fellers as 'lows to set right down and play off anything right away that can't make anything of the Flitterbat Lancers. That was two of 'em that was monkeyin' with me last night. They never could make anythin' of it at all, and I was tantalizing them with it all along till they got real mad, and reckoned to get it out o' my pocket and learn it at home. Ha, ha! So I got away for a bit, and just rolled it round a stone and heaved it through your winder before they could come up, your winder being the nearest one with a light in it. Ha, ha! I'll be considerable obliged you'll get it from your friend right now. Is he stayin' hereabout?"

The story was so ridiculously lame that I determined to confront my visitor with Hewitt, and observe the result. If he had succeeded in making any sense of the Flitterbat Lancers, the scene might be amusing. So I answered at once, "Yes; his office is on the floor below; he will probably be in at about this time. Come down with me."

We went down, and found Hewitt in his outer office. "This gentleman," I told him with a solemn intonation, "has come to ask for his piece of manuscript music, the Flitterbat Lancers. He is particularly proud of it, because nobody who tries to play it can make any sort of tune out of it, and it was entirely because two dear friends of his were anxious to drag it out of his pocket and practice it over on the quiet that he flung it through my windowpane last night, wrapped round a piece of concrete."

The stranger glanced sharply at me, and I could see that my manner and tone rather disconcerted him. Burt Hewitt came forward at once. "Oh, yes," he said "just so—quite a natural sort of thing. As a matter of fact, I quite expected you. Your umbrella's wet—do you mind putting it in the stand? Thank you. Come into my private office."

We entered the inner room, and Hewitt, turning to the stranger, went on: "Yes, that is a very extraordinary piece of music, that Flitterbat Lancers. I have been having a little bit of practice with it myself, though I'm really nothing of a musician. I don't wonder you are anxious to keep it to yourself. Sit down."

The stranger, with a distrustful look at Hewitt, complied. At this moment, Hewitt's clerk, Kerrett, entered from the outer office with a slip of paper. Hewitt glanced at it, and crumpled it in his hand. "I am engaged just now," was his remark, and Kerrett vanished.

"And now," Hewitt said, as he sat down and suddenly turned to the stranger with an intent gaze, "and now, Mr Hoker, we'll talk of this music."

The stranger started and frowned. "You've the advantage of me, sir," he said; "you seem to know my name, but I don't know yours."

Hewitt smiled pleasantly. "My name," he said, "is Hewitt, Martin Hewitt, and it is my business to know a great many things. For instance, I know that you are Mr Reuben B. Hoker, of Robertsville, Ohio."

The visitor pushed his chair back, and stared. "Well—that gits me," he said. "You're a pretty smart chap, Mr Hewitt. I've heard your name before, of course. And—and so you've been a-studyin' the Flitterbat Lancers, have you?" This with a keen glance at Hewitt's face. "Well, s'pose you have. What's your idea?"

"Why," answered Hewitt, still keeping his steadfast gaze on Hoker's eyes, "I think it's pretty late in the century to be fishing about for the Wedlake jewels."

These words astonished me almost as much as they did Mr Hoker. The great Wedlake jewel robbery is, as many will remember, a traditional story of the 'sixties. I remembered no more of it at the time than probably most men do who have at some time or another read the causes celèbres of the century. Sir Francis Wedlake's country house had been robbed, and the whole of Lady Wedlake's magnificent collection of jewels stolen. A man named Shiels, a strolling musician, had been arrested and had been sentenced to a long term of penal servitude. Another man named Legg—one of the comparatively wealthy scoundrels who finance promising thefts or swindles and pocket the greater part of the proceeds—had also been punished, but only a very few of the trinkets, and those quite unimportant items, had been recovered. The great bulk of the booty was never brought to light. So much I remembered, and Hewitt's sudden mention of the Wedlake jewels in connection with my broken window, Mr Reuben B. Hoker, and the Flitterbat Lancers, astonished me not a little.

As for Hoker, he did his best to hide his perturbation, but with little success. "Wedlake jewels, eh?" he said; "and—and what's that to do with it, anyway?"

"To do with it?" responded Hewitt, with an air of carelessness. "Well, well, I had my idea, nothing more. If the Wedlake jewels have nothing to do with it, we'll say no more about it, that's all. Here's your paper, Mr Hoker—only a little crumpled." He rose and placed the article in Mr Hoker's hand, with the manner of terminating the interview.

Hoker rose, with a bewildered look on his face, and turned toward the door. Then he stopped, looked at the floor, scratched his cheek, and finally sat down and put his hat on the ground. "Come," he said, "we'll play a square game. That paper has something to do with the Wedlake jewels, and, win or lose, I'll tell you all I know about it. You're a smart man and whatever I tell you, I guess it won't do me no harm; it ain't done me no good yet, anyway."

"Say what you please, of course," Hewitt answered, "but think first. You might tell me something you'd be sorry for afterward."

"Say, will you listen to what I say, and tell me if you think I've been swindled or not? My two hundred and fifty dollars is gone now, and I guess I won't go skirmishing after it anymore if you think it's no good. Will you do that much?"

"As I said before," Hewitt replied, "tell me what you please, and if I can help you I will. But remember, I don't ask for your secrets."

"That's all right, I guess, Mr Hewitt. Well, now, it was all like this." And Mr Reuben B. Hoker plunged into a detailed account of his adventures since his arrival in London.

Relieved of repetitions, and put as directly as possible, it was as follows: Mr Hoker was a wagon-builder, had made a good business from very humble beginnings, and intended to go on and make it still a better. Meantime, he had come over to Europe for a short holiday—a thing he had promised himself for years. He was wandering about the London streets on the second night after his arrival in the city, when he managed to get into conversation with two men at a bar. They were not very prepossessing men, though flashily dressed. Very soon they suggested a game of cards. But Reuben B. Hoker was not to be had in that way, and after a while, they parted. The two were amusing enough fellows in their way, and when Hoker saw them again the next night in the same bar, he made no difficulty in talking with them freely. After a succession of drinks, they told him that they had a speculation on hand—a speculation that meant thousands if it succeeded—and to carry out which they were only waiting for a paltry sum of £50. There was a house, they said, in which was hidden a great number of jewels of immense value, which had been deposited there by a man who was now dead. Exactly in what part of the house the jewels were to be found they did not know. There was a paper, they said, which was supposed to contain some information, but as yet they hadn't been quite able to make it out. But that would really matter very little if once they could get possession of the house. Then they would simply set to work and search from the topmost chimney to the lowermost brick, if necessary. The only present difficulty was that the house was occupied, and that the landlord wanted a large deposit of rent down before he would consent to turn out his present tenants and give them possession at a higher rental. This deposit would come to £50, and they hadn't the money. However, if any friend of theirs who meant business would put the necessary sum it their disposal, and keep his mouth shut, they would make him an equal partner in the proceeds with themselves; and as the value of the whole haul would probably be something not very far off £20,000, the speculation would bring a tremendous return to the man who w as smart enough to put down his £50.

Hoker, very distrustful, skeptically demanded more detailed particulars of the scheme. But these the two men (Luker and Birks were their names, he found, in course of talking) inflexibly refused to communicate.

"Is it likely," said Luker, "that we should give the 'ole thing away to anybody who might easily go with his fifty pounds and clear out the bloomin' show? Not much. We've told you what the game is, and if you'd like to take a flutter with your fifty, all right; you'll do as well as anybody, and we'll treat you square. If you don't—well, don't, that's all. We'll get the oof from somewhere—there's blokes as 'ud jump at the chance. Anyway, we ain't going to give the show away before you've done somethin' to prove you're on the job, straight. Put your money in, and you shall know as much as we do."

Then there were more drinks, and more discussion. Hoker was still reluctant, though tempted by the prospect, and growing more venturesome with each drink.

"Don't you see," said Birks, "that if we was a-tryin' to 'ave you we should out with a tale as long as yer arm, all complete, with the address of the 'ouse and all. Then I s'pose you'd lug out the pieces on the nail, without askin' a bloomin' question. As it is, the thing's so perfectly genuine that we'd rather lose the chance and wait for some other bloke to find the money than run a chance of givin' the thing away. It's a matter o' business, simple and plain, that's all. It's a question of either us trustin' you with a chance of collarin' twenty thousand pounds or you trustin' us with a paltry fifty. We don't lay out no 'igh moral sentiments, we only say the weight o' money is all on one side. Take it or leave it, that's all. 'Ave another Scotch?"

The talk went on and the drinks went on, and it all ended, at "chucking-out time," in Reuben B. Hoker handing over five £10 notes, with smiling, though slightly incoherent, assurances of his eternal friendship for Luker and Birks.

In the morning he awoke to the realization of a bad head, a bad tongue, and a bad opinion of his proceedings of the previous night. In his sober senses it seemed plain that he had been swindled. All day he cursed his fuddled foolishness, and at night he made for the bar that had been the scene if the transaction, with little hope of seeing either Luker or Birks, who had agreed to be there to meet him. There they were, however, and, rather to his surprise, they made no demand for more money. They asked him if he understood music, and showed him the worn old piece of paper containing the Flitterbat Lancers. The exact spot, they said, where the jewels were hidden was supposed to be indicated somehow on that piece of paper. Hoker did not understand music, and could find nothing on the paper that looked in the least like a direction to a hiding-place for jewels or anything else.

Luker and Birks then went into full particulars of their project. First, as to its history. The jewels were the famous Wedlake jewels, which had been taken from Sir Francis Wedlake's house in 1866 and never heard of again. A certain Jerry Shiels had been arrested in connection with the robbery, had been given a long sentence of penal servitude, and had died in jail. This Jerry Shiels was an extraordinarily clever criminal, and travelled about the country as a street musician. Although an expert burglar, he very rarely perpetrated robberies himself, but acted as a sort of traveling fence, receiving stolen property and transmitting it to London or out of the country. He also acted as the agent of a man named Legg, who had money, and who financed any likely looking project of a criminal nature that Shiels might arrange.

Jerry Shiels traveled with a "pardner"—a man who played the harp and acted as his assistant and messenger in affairs wherein Jerry was reluctant to appear personally. When Shiels was arrested, he had in his possession a quantity of printed and manuscript music, and after his first remand his "pardner," Jimmy Snape, applied for the music to be given up to him, in order, as he explained, that he might earn his living. No objection was raised to this, and Shiels was quite willing that Snape should have it, and so it was handed over. Now among the music was a small slip, headed Flitterbat Lancers, which Shiels had shown to Snape before the arrest. In case of Shiels being taken, Snape was to take this slip to Legg as fast as he could.

But as chance would have it, on that very day Legg himself was arrested, and soon after was sentenced also to a term of years. Snape hung about in London for a little while, and then emigrated. Before leaving, however, he gave the slip of music to Luker's father, a rag-shop keeper, to whom he owed money. He explained its history, and Luker senior made all sorts of fruitless efforts to get at the information concealed in the paper. He had held it to the fire to bring out concealed writing, had washed it, had held it to the light till his eyes ached, had gone over it with a magnifying glass—all in vain. He had got musicians to strum out the notes on all sorts of instruments—backwards, forwards, alternately, and in every other way he could think of. If at any time he fancied a resemblance in the resulting sound to some familiar song-tune, he got that song and studied all its words with loving care, upside-down, right-side up—every way. He took the words Flitterbat Lancers and transposed the letters in all directions, and did everything else he could think of. In the end he gave it up, and died. Now, lately, Luker junior had been impelled with a desire to see into the matter. He had repeated all the parental experiments, and more, with the same lack of success. He had taken his "pal" Birks into his confidence, and together they had tried other experiments till at last they began to believe that the message had probably been written in some sort of invisible ink which the subsequent washings had erased altogether. But he had done one other thing: he had found the house which Shiels had rented at the time of his arrest, and in which a good quantity of stolen property—not connected with the Wedlake case—was discovered. Here, he argued, if anywhere, Jerry Shiels had hidden the jewels. There was no other place where he could be found to have lived, or over which he had sufficient control to warrant his hiding valuables therein. Perhaps, once the house could be properly examined, something about it might give a clue as to what the message of the Flitterbat Lancers meant.

Hoker, of course, was anxious to know where the house in question stood, but this Luker and Birks would on no account inform him. "You've done your part," they said, "and now you leave us to do ours. There's a bit of a job about gettin' the tenants out. They won't go, and it'll take a bit of time before the landlord can make them. So you just hold your jaw and wait. When we're safe in the 'ouse, and there's no chance of anybody else pokin' in, then you can come and help find the stuff."

Hoker went home that night sober, but in much perplexity. The thing might be genuine, after all; indeed, there were many little things that made him think it was. But then, if it were, what guarantee had he that he would get his share, supposing the search turned out successful? None at all. But then it struck him for the first time that these jewels, though they may have lain untouched so long, were stolen property after all. The moral aspect of the affair began to trouble him a little, but the legal aspect troubled him more. That consideration however, he decided to leave over for the present. He had no more than the word of Luker and Birks that the jewels (if they existed) were those of Lady Wedlake, and Luker and Birks themselves only professed to know from hearsay. At any rate, he made up his mind to have some guarantee for his money. In accordance with this resolve, he suggested, when he met the two men the next day, that he should take charge of the slip of music and make an independent study of it. This proposal, however, met with an instant veto.

Hoker resolved to make up a piece of paper, folded as like the slip of music as possible, and substitute one for the other at their next meeting. Then he would put the Flitterbat Lancers in some safe place, and face his fellow conspirators with a hand of cards equal to their own. He carried out his plan the next evening with perfect success, thanks to the contemptuous indifference with which Luker and Birks had begun to regard him. He got the slip in his pocket, and left the bar. He had not gone far, however, before Luker discovered the loss, and soon he became conscious of being followed. He looked for a cab, but he was in a dark street, and no cab was near. Luker and Birks turned the corner and began to run. He saw they must catch him. Everything now depended on his putting the Flitterbat Lancers out of their reach, but where he could himself recover it. He ran till he saw a narrow passageway on his right, and into this he darted. It led into a yard where stones were lying about, and in a large building before him he saw the window of a lighted room a couple of floors up. It was a desperate expedient, but there was no time for consideration. He wrapped a stone in the paper and flung it with all his force through the lighted window. Even as he did it he heard the feet of Luker and Birks as they hurried down the street. The rest of the adventure in the court I myself saw.

Luker and Birks kept Hoker in their lodgings all that night. They searched him unsuccessfully for the paper; they bullied, they swore, they cajoled, they entreated, they begged him to play the game square with his pals. Hoker merely replied that he had put the Flitterbat Lancers where they couldn't easily find it, and that he intended playing the game square as long as they did the same. In the end they released him, apparently with more respect than they had before entertained, advising him to get the paper into his possession as soon as he could.

"And now," said Mr Hoker, in conclusion of his narrative, "perhaps you'll give me a bit of advice. Am I playin' a fool-game running after these toughs, or ain't I?"

Hewitt shrugged his shoulders. "It all depends," he said, "on your friends Luker and Birks. They may want to swindle you, or they may not. I'm afraid they'd like to, at any rate. But perhaps you've got some little security in this piece of paper. One thing is plain: they certainly believe in the deposit of the jewels themselves, else they wouldn't have taken so much trouble to get the paper back."

"Then I guess I'll go on with the thing, if that's it."

"That depends, of course, on whether you care to take trouble to get possession of what, after all, is somebody else's lawful property."

Hoker looked a little uneasy. "Well," he said, "there's that, of course. I didn't know nothin' of that at first, and when I did I'd parted with my money and felt entitled to get something back for it. Anyway, the stuff ain't found yet. When it is, why then, you know, I might make a deal with the owner. But, say, how did you find out my name, and about this here affair being jined up with the Wedlake jewels?"

Hewitt smiled. "As to the name and address, you just think it over a little when you've gone away, and if you don't see how I did it. You're not so cute as I think you are. In regard to the jewels—well, I just read the message of the Flitterbat Lancers, that's all."

"You read it? Whew! And what does it say? How did you do it?" Hoker turned the paper over eagerly in his hands as he spoke.

"See, now," said Hewitt, "I won't tell you all that, but I'll tell you something, and it may help you to test the real knowledge of Luker and Birks. Part of the message is in these words, which you had better write down: Over the coals the fifth dancer slides, says Jerry Shield the homey.'"

"What?" Hoker exclaimed, "fifth dancer slides over the coals? That's mighty odd. What's it all about?"

"About the Wedlake jewels, as I said. Now you can go and make a bargain with Luker and Birks. The only other part of the message is an address, and that they already know, if they have been telling the truth about the house they intend taking. You can offer to tell them what I have told you of the message, after they have told you where the house is, and proved to you that they are taking the steps they talked of. If they won't agree to that, I think you had best treat them as common rogues and charge them with obtaining your money under false pretenses."

Nothing more would Hewitt say than that, despite Hoker's many questions; and when at last Hoker had gone, almost as troubled and perplexed as ever, my friend turned to me and said, "Now, Brett, if you haven't lunched and would like to see the end of this business, hurry!"

"The end of it?" I said. "Is it to end so soon? How?"

"Simply by a police raid on Jerry Shiels's old house with a search warrant. I communicated with the police this morning before I came here."

"Poor Hoker!" I said.

"Oh, I had told the police before I saw Hoker, or heard of him, of course. I just conveyed the message on the music slip—that was enough. But I'll tell you all a out it when there's more time; I must be off now. With the information I have given him, Hoker and his friends may make an extra push and get into the house soon, but I couldn't resist the temptation to give the unfortunate Hoker some sort of sporting chance—though it's a poor one, I fear. Get your lunch as quickly as you can, and go at once to Colt Row, Bankside—Southwark way, you know. Probably we shall be there before you. If not, wait."

Colt Row was not difficult to find. It was one of those places that decay with an excess of respectability, like Drury Lane and Clare Market. Once, when Jacob's Island was still an island, a little farther down the river, Colt Row had evidently been an unsafe place for a person with valuables about him, and then it probably prospered, in its own way. Now it was quite respectable, but very dilapidated and dirty. Perhaps it was sixty yards long—perhaps a little more. It was certainly a very few yards wide, and the houses at each side had a patient and forlorn look of waiting for a metropolitan improvement to come along and carry them away to their rest.

I could see no sign of Hewitt, nor of the police, so I walked up and down the narrow pavement for a little while. As I did so, I became conscious of a face at the window of the least ruinous house in the row, a face that I fancied expressed particular interest in my movements. The house was an old gabled structure, faced with plaster. What had apparently once been a shop-window on the ground floor was now shuttered up, and the face that watched me—an old woman's—looked out from the window above. I had noted these particulars with some curiosity, when, arriving again at the street corner, I observed Hewitt approaching, in company with a police inspector, and followed by two unmistakable plainclothesmen.

"Well," Hewitt said, "you're first here after all. Have you seen any more of our friend Hoker?"

"No, nothing."

"Very well—probably he'll be here before long, though."

The party turned into Colt Row, and the inspector, walking up to the door of the house with the shuttered bottom window, knocked sharply. There was no response, so he knocked again, equally in vain.

"All out," said the inspector.

"No," I said; "I saw a woman watching me from the window above not three minutes ago."

"Ho, ho!" the inspector replied. "That's so, eh? One of you—you, Johnson—step round to the back, will you?"

One of the plainclothesmen started off, and after waiting another minute or two the inspector began a thundering cannonade of knocks that brought every available head out of the window of every inhabited room in the Row. At this the woman opened the window, and began abusing the inspector with a shrillness and fluency that added a street-corner audience to that already congregated at the windows.

"Go away, you blaggards!" the lady said, "you ought to be 'orse-w'ipped, every one of ye! A-comin' 'ere a-tryin' to turn decent people out o' 'ouse and 'ome! Wait till my 'usband comes 'ome—'e'll show yer, ye mutton-cadgin' scoundrels! Payin' our rent reg'lar, and good tenants as is always been—and I'm a respectable married woman, that's what I am, ye dirty great cowards!"—this last word with a low, tragic emphasis.

Hewitt remembered what Hoker had said about the present tenants refusing to quit the house on the landlord's notice. "She thinks we've come from the landlord to turn her out," he said to the inspector. "We're not here from the landlord, you old fool!" the inspector said. "We don't want to turn you out. We're the police, with a search warrant, and you'd better let us in or you'll get into trouble."

"'Ark at 'im!" the woman screamed, pointing at the inspector. "'Ark at 'im! Thinks I was born yesterday, that feller! Go 'ome, ye dirty pie-stealer, go 'ome!"

The audience showed signs of becoming a small crowd, and the inspector's patience gave out. "Here, Bradley," he said, addressing the remaining plainclothesman, "give a hand with these shutters," and the two—both powerful men—seized the iron bar which held the shutters and began to pull. But the garrison was undaunted, and, seizing a broom, the woman began to belabour the invaders about the shoulders and head from above. But just at this moment, the woman, emitting a terrific shriek, was suddenly lifted from behind and vanished. Then the head of the plainclothesman who had gone round to the back appeared, with the calm announcement, "There's a winder open behind, sir. But I'll open the front door if you like."

In a minute the bolts were shot, and the front door swung back. The placid Johnson stood in the passage, and as we passed in he said, "I've locked 'er in the back room upstairs."

"It's the bottom staircase, of course," the inspector said; and we tramped down into the basement. A little way from the stair-foot Hewitt opened a cupboard door, which enclosed a receptacle for coals. "They still keep the coals here, you see," he said, striking a match and passing it to and fro near the sloping roof of the cupboard. It was of plaster, and covered the underside of the stairs.

"And now for the fifth dancer," he said, throwing the match away and making for the staircase again. "One, two, three, four, five," and he tapped the fifth stair from the bottom.

The stairs were uncarpeted, and Hewitt and the inspector began a careful examination of the one he had indicated. They tapped it in different places, and Hewitt passed his hands over the surfaces of both tread and riser. Presently, with his hand at the outer edge of the riser, Hewitt spoke. "Here it is, I think," he said; "it is the riser that slides."

He took out his pocketknife and scraped away the grease and paint from the edge of the old stair. Then a joint was plainly visible. For a long time the plank, grimed and set with age, refused to shift; but at last, by dint of patience and firm fingers, it moved, and was drawn clean out from the end.

Within, nothing was visible but grime, fluff, and small rubbish. The inspector passed his hand along the bottom angle. "Here's something," he said. It was the gold hook of an old-fashioned earring, broken off short.

Hewitt slapped his thigh. "Somebody's been here before us," he said "and a good time back too, judging from the dust. That hook's a plain indication that jewellery was here once. There's plainly nothing more, except—except this piece of paper." Hewitt's eyes had detected—black with loose grime as it was—a small piece of paper lying at the bottom of the recess. He drew it out and shook off the dust. "Why, what's this?" he exclaimed. "More music!"

We went to the window, and there saw in Hewitt's hand a piece of written musical notation, thus:—

Hewitt pulled out from his pocket a few pieces of paper. "Here is a copy I made this morning of the Flitterbat Lancers, and a note or two of my own as well," he said. He took a pencil, and, constantly referring to his own papers, marked a letter under each note on the last-found slip of music. When he had done this, the letters read:

You are a clever cove whoever you are but there was a cleverer says Jim Snape the horney's mate.

"You see." Hewitt said handing the inspector the paper. "Snape, the unconsidered messenger, finding Legg in prison, set to work and got the jewels for himself. The thing was a cryptogram, of course, of a very simple sort, though uncommon in design. Snape was a humorous soul, too, to leave this message here in the same cipher, on the chance of somebody else reading the Flitterbat Lancers."

"But," I asked, "why did he give that slip of music to Laker's father?"

"Well, he owed him money, and got out or it that way. Also, he avoided the appearance of 'flushness' that paying the debt might have given him, and got quietly out of the country with his spoils."

The shrieks upstairs had grown hoarser, but the broom continued vigorously. "Let that woman out," said the inspector, "and we'll go and report. Not much good looking for Snape now, I fancy. But there's some satisfaction in clearing up that old quarter-century mystery."

We left the place pursued by the execrations of the broom wielder, who bolted the door behind us, and from the window defied us to come back, and vowed she would have us all searched before a magistrate for what we had probably stolen. In the very next street we hove in sight of Reuben B. Hoker in the company of two swell-mob-looking fellows, who sheered off down a side turning in sight of our group. Hoker, too, looked rather shy at the sight of the inspector.

"The meaning of the thing was so very plain," Hewitt said to me afterwards, "that the duffers who had the Flitterbat Lancers in hand for so long never saw it at all. If Shiels had made an ordinary clumsy cryptogram, all letters and figures, they would have seen what it was at once, and at least would have tried to read it; but because it was put in the form of music, they tried everything else but the right way. It was a clever dodge of Shiels's, without a doubt. Very few people, police officers or not, turning over a heap of old music, would notice or feel suspicious of that little slip among the rest. But once one sees it is a cryptogram (and the absence of bar lines and of notes beyond the stave would suggest that) the reading is as easy as possible. For my part I tried it as a cryptogram at once. You know the plan—it has been described a hundred times. See here—look at this copy of the Flitterbat Lancers. Its only difficulty—and that is a small one—is that the words are not divided. Since there are positions for less than a dozen notes on the stave, and there are twenty-six letters to be indicated, it follows that crotchets, quavers, and semiquavers on the same line or space must mean different letters. The first step is obvious. We count the notes to ascertain which sign occurs most frequently, and we find that the crotchet in the top space is the sign required—it occurs no less than eleven times. Now the letter most frequently occurring in an ordinary sentence of English is e. Let us then suppose that this represents e. At once a coincidence strikes us. In ordinary musical notation in the treble clef the note occupying the top space would be E. Let us remember that presently.

"Now the most common word in the English language is 'the.' We know the sign for e, the last letter of this word, so let us see if in more than one place that sign is preceded by two others identical in each case. If so, the probability is that the other two signs will represent t and h, and the whole word will be 'the.' Now it happens in no less than four places the sign e is preceded by the same two other signs— once in the first line, twice in the second, and once in the fourth. No word of three letters ending in e would be in the least likely to occur four times in a short sentence except 'the.' Then we will call it 'the', and note the signs preceding the e. They are a quaver under the bottom line for the t, and a crotchet on the first space for the h. We travel along the stave, and wherever these signs occur we mark them with t or h, as the case may be.

"But now we remember that e, the crotchet in the top space, is in its right place as a musical note, while the crotchet in the bottom space means h, which is no musical note at all. Considering this for a minute, we remember that among the notes which are expressed in ordinary music on the treble stave, without the use of ledger lines, d, e and f are repeated at the lower and at the upper part of the stave. Therefore, anybody making a cryptogram of musical notes would probably use one set of these duplicate positions to indicate other letters, and as a is in the lower part of the stave, that is where the variation comes in. Let us experiment by assuming that all the crotchets above f in ordinary musical notation have their usual values, and let us set the letters over their respective notes. Now things begin to shape. Look toward the end of the second line: there is the word the and the letters f f t h, with another note between the two f's. Now that word can only possibly be fifth, so that now we have the sign for i. It is the crotchet on the bottom line. Let us go through and mark the i's.

"And now observe. The first sign of the lot is i, and there is one other sign before the word 'the.' The only words possible here beginning with i, and of two letters, are it, if, is and in. Now we have the signs for t and f, so we know that it isn't it or if. Is would be unlikely here, because there is a tendency, as you see, to regularity in these signs, and t, the next letter alphabetically to s, is at the bottom of the stave. Let us try n. At once we get the word dance at the beginning of line three. And now we have got enough to see the system of the thing. Make a stave and put G A B C and the higher D E F in their proper musical places. Then fill in the blank places with the next letters of the alphabet downward, h i j, and we find that h and i fall in the places we have already discovered for them as crotchets. Now take quavers, and go on with k l m n o, and so on as before, beginning on the A space. When you have filled the quavers, do the same with semiquavers—there are only six alphabetical letters left for this—u v w x y z. Now you will find that this exactly agrees with all we have ascertained already, and if you will use the other letters to fill up over the signs still unmarked you will get the whole message:

"In the Colt Row ken over the coals the fifth dancer slides says Jerry Shiels the horney.

"'Dancer,' as perhaps you didn't know, is thieves' slang for a stair, and 'horney' is the strolling musician's name for cornet player. Of course the thing took a little time to work out, chiefly because the sentence was short, and gave one few opportunities. But anybody with the key, using the cipher as a means of communication, would read it easily.

"As soon as I had read it, of course I guessed the purport of the Flitterbat Lancers. Jerry Shiels's name is well-known to anybody with half my knowledge of the criminal records of the century, and his connection with the missing Wedlake jewels, and his death in prison, came to my mind at once. Certainly here was something hidden, and as the Wedlake jewels seemed most likely, I made the shot in talking to Hoker."

"But you terribly astonished him by telling him his name and address. How was that?" I asked curiously.

Hewitt laughed aloud. "That," he said; "why, that was the thinnest trick of all. Why, the man had it engraved on the silver band of his umbrella handle. When he left his umbrella outside, Kerrett (I had indicated the umbrella to him by a sign) just copied the lettering on one of the ordinary visitors' forms, and brought it in. You will remember I treated it as an ordinary visitor's announcement." And Hewitt laughed again.

On the afternoon of the next day Reuben B. Hoker called on Hewitt and had half-an-hour's talk with him in his private room. After that he came up to me with half-a-crown in his hand. "Sir," he said, "everything has turned out a durned sell. I don't want to talk about it any more. I'm goin' out of this durn country. Night before last I broke your winder. You put the damage at half-a-crown. Here is the money. Good-day to you, sir."

And Reuben B. Hoker went out into the tumultuous world.

V. — THE CASE OF THE LATE MR. REWSE

I

Of this case I personally saw nothing beyond the first advent in Hewitt's office of Mr. Horace Bowyer, who put the case in his hands, and then I merely saw Mr. Bowyer's back as I passed down stairs from my rooms. But I noted the case in full detail after Hewitt's return from Ireland, as it seemed to me one not entirely without interest, if only as an exemplar of the fatal ease with which a man may unwittingly dig a pit for his own feet—a pit from which there is no climbing out.

A few moments after I had seen the stranger disappear into Hewitt's office, Kerrett brought to Hewitt in his inner room a visitor's slip announcing the arrival on argent business of Mr. Horace Bowyer. That the visitor was in a hurry was plain from a hasty rattling of the closed wicket in the outer room where Mr. Bowyer was evidently making impatient attempts to follow his announcement in person. Hewitt showed himself at the door and invited Mr. Bowyer to as soon as Kerrett had with much impetuosity florid gentleman with a loud voice and a large stare.

"Mr. Hewitt," he said, "I must claim your immediate attention to a business of the utmost gravity. Will you please consider yourself commissioned, wholly regardless of expense, to set aside whatever you may have in hand and devote yourself to the case I shall put in your hands?"

"Certainly not," Hewitt replied with a slight smile. "What I have in hand are matters which I have engaged to attend to, and no mere compensation for loss of fees could persuade me to leave my clients in the lurch, else what would prevent some other gentleman coming here to-morrow with a bigger fee than yours and bribing me away from you?"

"But this—this is a most serious thing, Mr. Hewitt. A matter of life or death—it is indeed!"

"Quite so," Hewitt replied; "but there are a thousand such matters at this moment pending of which you and I know nothing, and there are also two or three more of which you know nothing but on which I am at work. So that it becomes a question of practicability. If you will tell me your business I can judge whether or not I may be able to accept your commission concurrently with those I have in hand. Some operations take months of constant attention; some can be conducted intermittently; others still are a mere matter of a few days many of hours simply."

"I will tell you then," Mr. Bowyer replied. "In the first place, will you have the kindness to read that? It is a cutting from the Standard's column of news from the provinces of two days ago."

Hewitt took the cutting and read as follows:—

"The epidemic of small-pox in County Mayo, Ireland, shows few signs of abating. The spread of the disease has been very remarkable considering the widely-scattered nature of the population, though there can be no doubt that the market towns are the centres of infection, and that it is from these that the germs of contagion are carried into the country by people from all parts who resort thither on market days. In many cases the disease has assumed a particularly malignant form, and deaths have been very rapid and numerous. The comparatively few medical men available are sadly overworked, owing largely to the distances separating their different patients. Among those who have succumbed within the last few days is Mr. Algernon Rewse, a young English gentleman who has been staying with a friend at a cottage a few miles from Cullanin, on a fishing excursion."

Hewitt placed the cutting on the table at his side. "Yes?" he said inquiringly.

"It is to Mr. Algernon Rewse's death you wish to draw my attention?"

"It is," Mr. Bowyer answered; "and the reason I come to you is that I very much suspect—more than suspect, indeed—that Mr. Algernon Rewse has not died by smallpox, but has been murdered—murdered cold-bloodedly, and for the most sordid motives, by the friend who has been sharing his holiday."

"In what way do you suppose him to have been murdered?"

"That I cannot say—that, indeed, I want you to find out, among other things—chiefly perhaps, the murderer himself, who has made off."

"And your own status in the matter," queried Hewitt, "is that of—?"

"I am trustee under a will by which Mr. Rewse would have benefited considerably had he lived but a month or two longer. That circumstance indeed lies rather near the root of the matter. The thing stood thus. Under the will I speak of that of young Rewse's uncle, a very old friend of mine in his lifetime—the money lay in trust till the young fellow should attain twenty-five years of age. His younger sister, Miss Mary Rewse, was also benefited, but to a much smaller extent. She was to come into her property also on attaining the age of twenty-five, or on her marriage, whichever event happened first. It was further provided that in case either of these young people died before coming into the inheritance, his Or her share should go to the survivor: I want you particularly to remember this. You will observe that now, in consequence of young Algernon Rewse's death, barely two months before his twenty-fifth birthday, the whole of the very large property—all personalty, and free from any tie or restriction—which would otherwise have been his, will, in the regular course, pass, on her twenty=fifth birthday, or on her marriage, to Miss Mary Rewse, whose own legacy was comparatively trifling. You will understand the importance of this when I tell you that the man whom I suspect of causing Algernon Rewse's death, and who has been his companion on his otherwise lonely holiday, is engaged to be married to Miss Rewse."

Mr. Bowyer paused at this, but Hewitt only raised his eyebrows and nodded.

"I have never particularly liked the man," Mr. Bowyer went on. "He never seemed to have much to say for himself. I like a man who holds up his head and opens 'his mouth. I don't believe in the sort of modesty that he showed so much of-it isn't genuine, A man can't afford to be genuinely meek and retiring who has his way to make in the world—and he was clever enough to know that."

"He is poor, then?" Hewitt asked.

"Oh yes, poor enough. His name, by-the-bye, is Main Stanley Main—and he is a medical man. He hasn't been practising, except as assistant, since he became qualified, the reason being, I understand, that he couldn't afford to buy a good practice. He is the person who will profit by young Rewse's death—or at any rate who intended to; but we will see about that. As for Mary, poor girl, she wouldn't have lost her brother for fifty fortunes."

"As to the circumstances of the death, now?"

"Yes, yes, I am coming to that. Young Algernon Rewse, you must know, had rather run down in health, and Main persuaded him that he wanted a change. I don't know what it was altogether, but Rewse seemed to have been having his own little love troubles and that sort of thing, you know. He'd been engaged, I think, or very nearly so, and the young lady died, and so on. Well, as I said, he had run down and got into low health and spirits, and no doubt a change of some sort would have done him good. This Stanley Main always seemed to have a great influence over the poor boy—he was about four or five years older than Rewse—and somehow he persuaded him to go away, the two together, to some outlandish wilderness of a place in the West of. Ireland for salmon-fishing. It seemed to me at the time rather a ridiculous sort of place to go to, but Main had his way, and they went. There was a cottage—rather a good sort of cottage, I believe, for the district—which some friend of Main's, once a landowner in the district, had put up as a convenient box for salmon-fishing, and they rented it. Not long after they got there this epidemic of small-pox got about in the district—though that, I believe, has had little to do with poor young Rewse's death. All appeared to go well until a day over a week ago, when Mrs. Rewse received this letter from Main." Mr. Bowyer handed Martin Hewitt a letter, written in an irregular and broken hand, as though of a person writing under stress of extreme agitation. It ran thus:—

"My dear Mrs. Rewse,—" You will probably have heard through the newspapers—indeed I think Algernon has told you in his letters—that a very bad epidemic of small-pox is abroad in this district. I am deeply grieved to have to tell you that Algernon himself has taken the disease in a rather bad form. He showed the first symptoms to-day (Tuesday), and he is now in bed in the cottage. It is fortunate that I, as a medical man, happen to be on the spot, as the nearest local doctor is five miles off at Cullanin, and he is working and travelling night and day as it is. I have my little medicine chest with me, and can get whatever else is necessary from Cullanin, so that everything is being done for Algernon that is possible, and I hope to bring him up to scratch in good health soon, though of course the disease is a dangerous one. Pray don't unnecessarily alarm yourself, and don't think about coming over here, or anything of that sort. You can do no good, and will only run risk yourself. I will take care to let you know how things go on, so please don't attempt to come. The journey is long and would be very trying to you, and you would have no place to stay at nearer than Cullanin, which is quite a centre of infection. I will write again to-morrow.—Yours most sincerely,

"Stanley Main."

Not only did the handwriting of this letter show signs of agitation, but here and there words had been repeated, and sometimes a letter had been omitted. Hewitt placed the letter on the table by the newspaper cutting, and Mr. Bowyer proceeded.

"Another letter followed on the next day," he said, handing it to Hewitt as he spoke; "a short one, as you see; not written with quite such signs of agitation. It merely says that Rewse is very bad, and repeats the former entreaties that his mother will not think of going to him."

Hewitt glanced at the letter and placed it with the other, while Mr. Bowyer continued:

"Notwithstanding Main's persistent anxiety that she should stay at home, Mrs. Rewse, who was of course terribly worried about her only son, had almost made up her mind, in spite of her very delicate health, to start for Ireland, when she received a third letter announcing Algernon's death. Here it is. It is certainly the sort of letter that one might expect to be written in such circumstances, and yet there seems to me at least a certain air of disingenuousness about the wording. There are, as you see, the usual condolences, and so forth. The disease was of the malignant type, it says, which is terribly rapid in its action, often carrying off the patient even before the eruption has time to form. Then—and this is a thing I wish you especially to note—there is once more a repetition of his desire that neither the young man's mother nor his sister shall come to Ireland. The funeral must take place immediately, he says, under arrangements made by the local authorities, and before they could reach the spot. Now doesn't this obtrusive anxiety of his that no connection of young Rewse's should be near him during his illness, nor even at the funeral, strike you as rather singular?"

"Well, possibly it is; though it may easily be nothing but zeal for the health of Mrs. Rewse and her daughter. As a matter of fact what Main says is very plausible. They could do no sort of good in the circumstances, and might easily run into danger themselves, to say nothing of the fatigue of the journey and general nervous upset. Mrs. Rewse is in weak health, I think you said?"

"Yes, she's almost an invalid in fact; she is subject to heart disease. But tell me now, as an entirely impartial observer, doesn't it seem to you that there is a very forced, unreal sort of tone in all these letters?"

"Perhaps one may notice something of the sort, but fifty things may cause that. The case from the beginning may have been worse than he made it out. What ensued on the receipt of this letter?"

"Mrs. Rewse was prostrated, of course. Her daughter communicated with me as a friend of the family, and that is how I heard of the whole thing for the first time. I saw the letters, and it seemed to me, looking at all the circumstances of the case, that somebody at least ought to go over and make certain that everything was as it should be. Here was this poor young man, staying in a lonely cottage with the only man in the world who had any reason to desire his death, or any profit to gain by it, and he had a very great inducement indeed. Moreover he was a medical man, carrying his medicine chest with him, remember, as he says himself in his letter. In this situation Rewse suddenly dies, with nobody about him, so far as there is anything to show, but Main himself. As his medical attendant it would be Main who would certify and register the death, and no matter what foul play might have taken place he would be safe as long as nobody was on the spot to make searching inquiries might easily escape even then, in fact. When one man is likely to profit much by the death of another a doctor's medicine chest is likely to supply but too easy a means to his end."

"Did you say anything of your suspicions to the ladies?"

"Well—well I hinted perhaps—no more than hinted, you know. But they wouldn't hear of it—got indignant, and 'took on' as people call it, worse than ever, so that I had to smooth them over. But since it seemed somebody's duty to see into the matter a little more closely, and there seemed to be nobody to do it but myself, I started off that very evening by the night mail. I was in Dublin early the next morning and spent that day getting across Ireland. The nearest station was ten miles from Cullanin, and that, as you remember, was five miles from the cottage, so that I drove over on the morning of the following day. I must say Main appeared very much taken aback at seeing me. His manner was nervous and apprehensive, and made me more suspicious than ever. The body had been buried, of course, a couple of days or more. I asked a few rather searching questions about the illness, and so forth, and his answers became positively confused. He had burned the clothes that Rewse was wearing at the time the disease first showed itself, he said, as well as all the bedclothes, since there was no really efficient means of disinfection at hand.

"His story in the main was that he had gone off to Cullanin one morning on foot to see about a top joint of a fishing-rod that was to be repaired. When he returned early in the afternoon he found Algernon Rewse sickening of small-pox, at once put him to bed, and there nursed him till he died. I wanted to know, of course, why no other medical man had been called in. He said that there was only one available, and it was doubtful if he could have been got at even a day's notice, so overworked was he; moreover he said this man, with his hurry and over-strain, could never have given the patient such efficient attention as he himself, who had nothing else to do. After a while I put it to him plainly that it would at any rate have been more prudent to have had the body at least inspected by some independent doctor, considering the fact that he was likely to profit so largely by young Rewse's death, and I suggested that with an exhumation order it might not be too late now, as a matter of justice to himself. The effect of that convinced me. The man gasped and turned blue with terror. It was a full minute, I should think, before he could collect himself sufficiently to attempt to dissuade me from doing what I had hinted at. He did so as soon as he could by every argument he could think of—entreated me in fact almost desperately.

"That decided me. I said that after what he had said, and particularly in view of his whole manner and bearing, I should insist, by every means in my power, on having the body properly examined, and I went off at once to Cullanin to set the telegraph going, and see whatever local authority might be proper. When I returned in the afternoon Stanley Main had packed his bag and vanished, and I have not heard nor seen anything of him since. I stayed in the neighbourhood that day and the next, and left for London in the evening. By the help of my solicitors proper representations were made at the Home Office, and, especially in view of Main's flight, a prompt order was made for exhumation and medical examination preliminary to an inquest. I am expecting to hear that the disinterment has been effected to-day. What I want you to do of course is chiefly to find Main. The Irish constabulary in that district are fine big men, and no doubt most excellent in quelling a faction fight or shutting up a shebeen, but I doubt their efficiency in anything requiring much more finesse. Perhaps also you may be able to find out something of the means by which the murder—it is plain it is one—was committed. It is quite possible that Main may have adopted some means to give the body the appearance, even to a medical man, of death from small-pox."

"That," Hewitt said, "is scarcely likely, else, indeed, why did he not take care that another doctor should see the body before the burial? That would have secured him. But that is not a thing one can deceive a doctor over. Of course in the circumstances exhumation is desirable, but if the case is one of smallpox, I don't envy the medical man who is to examine. At any rate the business is, I should imagine, not likely to be a very long one, and I can take it in hand at once. I will leave to-night for Ireland by the 6.30 train from Euston."

"Very good. I shall go over myself, of course. If anything comes to my knowledge in the meanwhile, of course I'll let you know."

An hour or two after this a cab stopped at the door, and a young lady dressed in black sent in her name and a minute later was shown into Hewitt's room. It was Miss Mary Rewse. She wore a heavy veil, and all she said she uttered in evidently deep distress of mind. Hewitt did what he could to calm her, and waited patiently.

At length she said: "I felt that I must come to you, Mr. Hewitt, and yet now that I am here I don't know what to say. Is it the fact that Mr. Bowyer has commissioned you to investigate the circumstances of my poor brother's death, and to discover the whereabouts of Mr. Main?"

"Yes, Miss Rewse, that is the fact. Can you tell me anything that will help me?"

"No, no, Mr. Hewitt, I fear not. But it is such a dreadful thing, and Mr. Bowyer is—I'm afraid he is so much prejudiced against Mr. Main that I felt I ought to do something—to say something at least to prevent you entering on the case with your mind made up that he has been guilty of such an awful thing. He is really quite incapable of it, I assure you."

"Pray, Miss Rewse," Hewitt replied, "don't allow that apprehension to disturb you. If Mr. Main is, as you say, incapable of such an act as perhaps he is suspected of, you may rest assured no harm will come to him. So far as I am concerned at any rate I enter the case with a perfectly open mind. A man in my profession who accepted prejudices at the beginning of a case would have very poor results to show indeed. As yet I have no opinion, no theory, no prejudice—nothing indeed but a bare outline of fads. I shall derive no opinion and no theory from anything but a consideration of the actual circumstances and evidences on the spot. I quite understand the relation in which Mr. Main stands in regard to yourself and your family Have you heard from him lately?"

"Not since the letter informing us of my brother's death."

"Before then?"

Miss Rewse hesitated.

"Yes," she said, "we corresponded. But—but there was really nothing—the letters were of a personal and private sort—they were—"

"Yes, yes, of course," Hewitt answered, with his eyes fixed keenly on the veil which Miss Rewse still kept down. "Of course I understand that. Then there is nothing else you can tell me?"

"No, I fear not. I can only implore you to remember that no matter what you may see and hear, no matter what the evidence may be, I am sure, sure, sure that poor Stanley could never do such a thing." And Miss Rewse buried her face in her hands.

Hewitt kept his eyes on the lady, though he smiled slightly, and asked, "How long have you known Mr. Main?"

"For some five or six years now. My poor brother knew him at school, though of course they were in different forms, Mr. Main being the elder."

"Were they always on good terms?"

"They were always like brothers."

Little more was said. Hewitt condoled with Miss Rewse as well as he might, and she presently took her departure. Even as she descended the stairs a messenger came with a short note from Mr. Bowyer enclosing a telegram just received from Cullanin. The telegram ran thus:—

BODY EXHUMED. DEATH FROM SHOT-WOUND. NO TRACE OF SMALL-POX. NOTHING YET HEARD OF MAIN. HAVE COMMUNICATED WITH CORONER.—O'REILLY.

II

Hewitt and Mr. Bowyer travelled towards Mayo together, Mr. Bowyer restless and loquacious on the subject of the business in hand, and Hewitt rather bored thereby. He resolutely declined to offer an opinion on any single detail of the case till he had examined the available evidence, and his occasional remarks on matters of general interest, the scenery and so forth, struck his companion, unused to business of the sort which had occasioned the journey, as strangely cold-blooded and indifferent. Telegrams had been sent ordering that no disarrangement of the contents of the cottage was to be allowed pending their arrival, and Hewitt well knew that nothing more was practicable till the site was reached. At Ballymaine, where the train was left at last, they stayed for the night, and left early the next morning for Cullanin, where a meeting with Dr. O'Reilly at the mortuary had been appointed. There the body lay stripped of its shroud, calm and gray, and beginning to grow ugly, with a scarcely noticeable breach in the flesh of the left breast.

"The wound has been thoroughly cleansed, closed and stopped with a carbolic plug before interment," Dr. O'Reilly said. He was a middle-aged, grizzled man, with a face whereon many recent sleepless nights had left their traces. "I have not thought it necessary to do anything in the way of dissection. The bullet is not present, it has passed clean through the body, between the ribs both back and front, piercing the heart on its way. The death must have been instantaneous."

Hewitt quickly examined the two wounds, back and front, as the doctor turned the body over, and then asked: "Perhaps, Dr. O'Reilly, you have had some experience of a gunshot wound before this?"

The doctor smiled grimly. "I think so," he answered, with just enough of brogue in his words to hint his nationality and no more. "I was an army surgeon for a good many years before I came to Cullanin, and saw service in Ashanti and in India."

"Come then," Hewitt said, "you're an expert. Would it have been possible for the shot to have been fired from behind?"

"Oh, no. See! the bullet entering makes a wound of quite a different character from that of the bullet leaving."

"Have you any idea of the weapon used?"

"A large revolver, I should think; perhaps of the regulation size; that is, I should judge the bullet to have been a conical one of about the size fitted to such a weapon—smaller than that from a rifle."

"Can you form an idea of from what distance the shot was fired?"

Dr. O'Reilly shook his head. "The clothes have all been burned," he said, "and the wound has been washed, otherwise one might have looked for powder blackening."

"Did you know either the dead man or Dr. Main personally?"

"Only very slightly. I may say I saw just such a pistol as might cause that sort of wound in his hands the day before he gave out that Rewse had been attacked by smallpox. I drove past the cottage as he stood in the doorway with it in his hand. He had the breach opened, and seemed to be either loading or unloading it—which it was I couldn't say."

"Very good, doctor, that may be important. Now is there any single circumstance, incident or conjecture that you can tell me of in regard to this case that you have not already mentioned?"

Doctor O'Reilly thought for a moment, and replied in the negative.

"I heard of course," he said, "of the reported new case of small-pox, and that Main had taken the case in hand himself. I was indeed relieved to hear it, for I had already more on my hands than one man can safely be expected to attend to. The cottage was fairly isolated, and there could have been nothing gained by removal to an asylum—indeed there was practically no accommodation. So far as I can make out nobody seems to have seen young Rewse, alive or dead, after Main had announced that he had the small-pox. He seems to have done everything himself, laying out the body and all, and you may be pretty sure that none of the strangers about was particularly anxious to have anything to do with it. The undertaker (there is only one here, and he is down with the small-pox himself now) was as much overworked as I was myself, and was glad enough to send off a coffin by a market cart and leave the laying out and screwing down to Main, since he had got those orders. Main made out the death certificate himself, and, since he was trebly qualified, everything seemed in order."

"The certificate merely attributed the death to small-pox, I take it, with no qualifying remarks?"

"Small-pox simply."

Hewitt and Mr. Bowyer bade Dr. O'Reilly good morning, and their car was turned in the direction of the cottage where Algernon Rewse had met his death. At the Town Hall in the market place, however, Hewitt stopped the car and set his watch by the public clock. "This is more than half an hour before London time," he said, "and we mustn't be at odds with the natives about the time."

As he spoke Dr. O'Reilly came running up breathlessly. "I've just heard something," he said. "Three men heard a shot in the cottage as they were passing, last Tuesday week."

"Where are the men?"

"I don't know at the moment; but they can be found. Shall I set about it?"

"If you possibly can," Hewitt said, "you will help us enormously. Can you send them messages to be at the cottage as soon as they can get there to-day? Tell them they shall have half-a-sovereign apiece."

"Right, I will. Good-day."

"Tuesday week," said Mr. Bowyer as they drove off; "that was the date of Main's first letter, and the day on which, by his account, Rewse was taken ill. Then if that was the shot that killed Rewse he must have been lying dead in the place while Main was writing those letters reporting his sickness to his mother. The cold-blooded scoundrel!"

"Yes," Hewitt replied, "I think it probable in any case that Tuesday was the day that Rewse was shot. It wouldn't have been safe for Main to write the mother lying letters about the small-pox before. Rewse might have written home in the meantime, or something might have occurred to postpone Main's plans, and then there would be impossible explanations required."

Over a very bad road they jolted on and in the end arrived where the road, now become a mere path, passed a tumble-down old farmhouse.

"This is where the woman lives who cooked and cleaned house for Rewse and Main," Mr. Bowyer said. "There is the cottage, scarce a hundred yards off, a little to the right of the track."

"Well," replied Hewitt, "suppose we stop here and ask her a few questions? I like to get the evidence of all the witnesses as soon as possible. It simplifies subsequent work wonderfully."

They alighted, and Mr. Bowyer roared through the open door and tapped with his stick. In reply to his summons a decent-looking woman of perhaps fifty, but wrinkled beyond her age, and better dressed than any woman Hewitt had seen since leaving Cullanin, appeared from the hinder buildings and curtsied pleasantly.

"Good morning, Mrs. Hurley, good morning," Mr. Bowyer said, "this is Mr. Martin Hewitt, a gentleman from London, who is going to look into this shocking murder of our young friend Mr. Rewse and sift it to the bottom. He would like you to tell him something, Mrs. Hurley."

The woman curtsied again. "An' it's the jintleman is welcome, sor, sad doin's as ut is." She had a low, pleasing voice, much in contrast with her unattractive appearance, and characterised by the softest and broadest brogue imaginable. "Will ye not come in? Mother av Hiven! An' thim two livin' together, an' fishin' an' readin' an' all, like brothers! An' trut' ut is he was a foine young jintleman indade, indade!"

"I suppose, Mrs. Hurley," Hewitt said, "you've seen as much of the life of those two gentlemen here as anybody?"

"True ut is, sor; none more—nor as much."

"Did you ever hear of anybody being on bad terms with Mr. Rewse—anybody at all, Mr. Main or another?"

"Niver a soul in all Mayo. How could ye? Such a foine young jintleman, an' fair-spoken an' all."

"Tell me all that happened on the day that you heard that Mr. Rewse was ill—Tuesday week."

"In the mornin', sor, 'twas much as ord'nary. I was over there at half afther sivin, an' 'twas half an hour afther that I cud hear the jintleman dhressin'. They tuk their breakfast—though Mr. Rewse's was a small wan. It was half afther nine that Mr. Main wint off walkin' to Cullanin, Mr. Rewse stayin' in, havin' letthers to write. Half an hour later I came away mesilf. Later than that (it was nigh elivin) I wint across for a pail from the yard, an' then, through the windy as I passed I saw the dear young jintleman sittin' writin' at the table calm an' peaceful—an' saw him no more in this warrl'."

"And after that?"

"Afther that, sor, I came back wid the pail, an' saw nor heard no more till two o'clock, whin Mr. Main came back from Cullanin."

"Did you see him as he came back?"

"That I did, sor, as I stud there nailin' the fence where the pig bruk ut. I'd been there an' had me of down the road lookin' for him an hour past, expectin' he might be bringin' somethin' for me to cook for their dinner. An' more by token he gave me the toime from his watch, set by the Town Hall clock."

"And was it two o'clock?"

"It was that to the sthroke, an' me own ould clock was right too whin I wint to set ut. An'—"

"One moment; may I see your clock?"

Mrs. Hurley turned and shut an open door which had concealed an old hanging clock. Hewitt produced his watch and compared the time. "Still right I see, Mrs. Hurley," he said; "your clock, keeps excellent time."

"It does that, sor, an' nivir more than claned twice by Rafferty since me own father (rest his soul!) lift ut here. 'Tis no bad clock, as Mr. Rewse himsilf said oft an' again; an' I always kape ut by the Town Hall toime. But as I was sayin', Mr. Main came back an' gave me the toime; thin he wint sthraight to his house, an' no more av him I saw till may be half afther three."

"And then?"

"An' thin, sor, he came across in a sad Lakin', wid a letther. 'Take ut,' sez he, 'an' have ut posted at Cullanin by the first that can get there. Mr. Rewse has the sickness on him awful bad,' he sez, 'an' ye must not be near the place or ye'll take ut. I have him to bed, an' his clothes I shall burn behin' the cottage,' sez he, 'so if ye see smoke ye'll know what ut is. There'll be no docthor wanted. I'm wan mesilf, an' I'll do all for 'um. An' sure I knew him for a docthor ivir since he come. 'The cottage ye shall not come near,' he sez, 'till ut's over one way or another, an' yez can lave whativir av food an' dhrink we want mid-betwixt the houses an' go back, an' I'll come and fetch ut. But have the letther posted,' he sez, 'at wanst. 'Tis not contagious,' he sez, 'bein' as I've dishinfected it mesilf. But kape yez away from the cottage.' An' I kept."

"And then did he go back to the cottage at once?"

"He did that, sor, an' a sore stew was he in to all seemin'—white as paper, and much need, too, the murtherin' Scutt! An' him always so much the jintleman an' all. Well I saw no more av him that day. Next day he laves another letther wid the dirtily' plates there mid-betwixt the houses, an' shouts for ut to be posted. 'Twas for the poor young jintleman's mother, sure, as was the other wan. An' the day afther there was another letther, an' wan for the undhertaker, too, for he tells me it's all over, an' he's dead. An' they buried him next day followin'.'"

"So that from the time you went for the pail and saw Mr. Rewse writing, till after the funeral, you were never at the cottage at all?"

"Nivir, sor; an' can ye blame me? Wid children an' Terence himself sick wid bronchitis in this house?"

"Of course, of course, you did quite right—indeed you only obeyed orders. But now think; do you remember on any one of those three days hearing a shot, or any other unusual noise in the cottage?"

"Nivir at all, sor. 'Tis that I've been thryin' to bring to mind these four days. Such may have been, but not that I heard."

"After you went for the pail, and before Mr. Main returned to the house, did Mr. Rowse leave the cottage at all, or might he have done so?"

"He did not lave at all, to my knowledge. Sure he might have gone an' he might have come back widout my knowin'. But see him I did not."

"Thank you, Mrs. Hurley. I think we'll go across to the cottage now. If any people come will you send them after us? I suppose a policeman is there?"

"He is, sor. An' the serjint is not far away. They've been in chyarge since Mr. Bowyer wint away last—but shlapin' here."

Hewitt and Mr. Bowyer walked towards the cottage. "Did you notice," said Mr. Bowyer, "that the woman saw Rewse writing letters? Now what were those letters, and where are they? He has no correspondents that I know of but his mother and sister, and they heard nothing from him. Is this something else?—some other plot? There is something very deep here."

"Yes," Hewitt replied thoughtfully, "I think our inquiries may take us deeper than we have 'expected; and in the matter of those letters—yes, I think they may he near the kernel of the mystery."

Here they arrived at the cottage—an uncommonly substantial structure for the district. It was square, of plain, solid brick, with a slated roof. On the patch of ground behind it there were still signs of the fires wherein Main had burnt Rewse's clothes and other belongings. And sitting on the window-sill in front was a big member of the R.I.C., soldierly and broad, who rose as they came and saluted Mr. Bowyer.

"Good-day, constable," Mr. Bowyer said. "I hope nothing has been disturbed?"

"Not a shtick, sor. Nobody's as much as gone in."

"Have any of the windows been opened or shut?" Hewitt asked.

"This wan was, sor," the policeman said, indicating the one behind him, "when they took away the corrpse, an' so was the next round the corrner. 'Tis the bedroom windier they are, an' they opened thim to give ut a bit av air. The other windy behin'—sittin'-room windy—has not been opened."

"Very well," Hewitt answered, "we'll take a look at that unopened window from the inside."

The door was opened and they passed inside. There was a small lobby, and on the left of this was the bedroom with two single beds. The only other room of consequence was the sitting-room, the cottage consisting merely of these, a small scullery and a narrow closet used as a bath-room, wedged between the bedroom and the sitting-room. They made for the single window of the sitting-room at the back. It was an ordinary sash window, and was shut, but the catch was not fastened. Hewitt examined the catch, drawing Mr. Bowyer's attention to a bright scratch on the grimy brass. "See," he said, "that nick in the catch exactly corresponds with the narrow space between the two frames of the window. And look"— he lifted the bottom sash a little as he spoke—"there is the mark of a knife on the frame of the top sash. Somebody has come in by that window, forcing the catch with a knife."

"Yes, yes!" cried Mr. Bowyer, greatly excited, "and he has gone out that way too, else why is the window shut and the catch not fastened? Why should he do that? What in the world does this thing mean?"

Before Hewitt could reply the constable put his head into the room and announced that one Larry Shanahan was at the door, and had been promised half-a-sovereign.

"One of the men who heard a shot," Hewitt said to Mr. Bowyer. "Bring him in, constable."

The constable brought in Larry Shanahan, and Larry Shanahan brought in a strong smell of whisky. He was an extremely ragged person, with only one eye, which caused him to hold his head aside as he regarded Hewitt, much as a parrot does. On his face sun-scorched brown and fiery red struggled for mastery, and his voice was none of the clearest. He held his hat against his stomach with one hand and with the other pulled his forelock.

"An' which is the honourable jintleman," he said, "as do be burrnin' to prisint me wid a bit o' goold?"

"Here I am," said Hewitt, jingling money in his pocket, "and here is the half-sovereign. It's only waiting where it is till you have answered a few questions. They say you heard a shot fired hereabout?"

"Faith, an' that I did, sor. 'Twas a shot in this house, indade, no other."

"And when was it?"

"Sure, 'twas in the afthernoon."

"But on what day?"

"Last Tuesday sivin-noight, sor, as I know by rayson av Ballyshiel fair that I wint to."

"Tell me all about it."

"I will, sor. 'Twas pigs I was dhrivin' that day, sor, to Ballyshiel fair from just beyond Cullanin, sor, I dhropped in wid Danny Mulcahy, that intentioned thravellin' the same way, an' while we tuk a thrifle av a dhrink in comes Dennis Grady, that was to go to Ballyshiel similarously. An' so we had another thrifle av a dhrink, or maybe a thrifle more, an' we wint togedther, passin' this way, sor, as ye may not know, bein' likely a shtranger. Well, sor, ut was as we were just forninst this place that there came a divil av a bang that makes us shtop simultaneous. 'What's that?' sez Dan. 'Tis a gunshot,' sez I, an' 'tis in the brick house too.' 'That is so,' sez Dennis; 'nowhere else.' And we lukt at wan another. 'An' what'll we do?' sez I. 'What would yez?' sez Dan; 'Tis none av our business.' 'That is so,' sez Dennis again, and we wint on. Ut was quare, maybe, but it might aisily be wan av the jiritlemen emptyin' a barr'l out o' windy or what not. An'—an' so—an' so Mr. Shanahan scratched his ear, an' so—we wint."

"And do you know at what time this was?"

Larry Shanahan ceased scratching, and seized his ear between thumb and forefinger, gazing severely at the floor with his one eye as he did so, plunged in computation. "Sure," he said, "'twould be—'twould be—let's see—'twould be—" he looked up, "'twould be half-past two maybe, or maybe a thrifle nearer three."

"And Main was in the place all the time after two," Mr. Bowyer said, bringing down his fist on his open hand. "That finishes it. We've nailed him to the minute."

"Had you a watch with you?" asked Hewitt.

"Divil of a watch in the company, sor. I made an internal calculation. 'Tis foive mile from Cullanin, and we never lift till near half an hour after the Town Hall clock had struck twelve. 'Twould take us two hours and a thrifle more, considherin' the pigs, an' the rough road, an' the distance, an' an' the thrifle of dhrink." His eye rolled slyly as he said it. "That was my calculation, sor."

Here the constable appeared with two more men. Each had the usual number of eyes, but in other respects they were very good copies of Mr. Shanahan. They were both ragged, and neither bore any violent likeness to a teetotaler. "Dan Mulcahy and Dennis Grady," announced the constable.

Mr. Dan Mulcahy's tale was of a piece with Mr. Larry Shanahan's, and Mr. Dennis Grady's was the same. They had all heard the shot it was plain. What Dan had said to Dennis and what Dennis had said to Larry mattered little. Also they were all agreed that the day was Tuesday by token of the fair. But as to the time of day there arose a disagreement.

"'Twas nigh soon afther wan o'clock," said Dan Mulcahy.

"Soon afther wan!" exclaimed Larry Shanahan with scorn. "Soon afther your grandmother's pig! 'Twas half afther two at laste. Ut sthruck twelve nigh half an hour before we lift Cullanin. Why, yez heard ut!"

"That I did not. Ut sthruck eleven, an' we wint in foive minutes."

"What fool-talk ye shpake Dan Mulcahy. 'Twas twelve sthruck; I counted ut."

"Thin ye counted wrong. I counted ut, an' 'twas elivin."

"Yez nayther av yez right," interposed Dennis Grady. "'Twas not elivin when we lift; 'twas not, be the mother av Moses!"

"I wondher at ye, Dennis Grady; ye must have been dhrunk as a Kerry cow," and both Mulcahy and Shanahan turned upon the obstinate Grady, and the dispute waxed clamorous till Hewitt stopped it.

"Come, come," he said, "never mind the time then. Settle that between you after you've gone. Does either of you remember—not calculate, you know, but remember—the time you got to Ballyshiel?—the actual time by a clock—not a guess."

Not one of the three had looked at a clock at Ballyshiel.

"Do you remember anything about coming home again?"

They did not. They looked furtively at one another and presently broke into a grin.

"Ah! I see how that was," Hewitt said good-humouredly. "That's all now, I think. Come, it's ten shillings each, I think." And he handed over the money. The men touched their forelocks again, stowed away the money and prepared to depart. As they went Larry Shanahan stepped mysteriously back again and said in a whisper, "Maybe the jintlemen wud like me to kiss the book on ut? An' as to the toime—"

"Oh, no thank you," Hewitt laughed. "We take your word for it Mr. Shanahan." And Mr. Shanahan pulled his forelock again and vanished.

"There's nothing but confusion to be got from them," Mr. Bowyer remarked testily. "It's a mere waste of time."

"No, no, not a waste of time," Hewitt replied, "nor a waste of money. One thing is made pretty plain. That is that the shot was fired on Tuesday. Mrs. Hurley never noticed the report, but these three men were close by, and there is no doubt that they heard it. It's the only single thing they agree about at all. They contradict one another over everything else, but they agree completely in that. Of course I wish we could have got the exact time; but that can't be helped. As it is it is rather fortunate that they disagreed so entirely. Two of them are certainly wrong, and perhaps all three. In any case it wouldn't have been safe to trust to mere computation of time by three men just beginning to get drunk, who had no particular reason for remembering. But if by any chance they had agreed on the time we might have been led into a wrong track altogether by taking the thing as fact. But a gunshot is not such a doubtful thing. When three independent witnesses hear a gunshot together there can be little doubt that a shot has been fired. Now I think you'd better sit down. Perhaps you can find something to read. I'm about to make a very minute examination of this place, and it will probably bore you if you've nothing else to do."

But Mr. Bowyer would think of nothing but the business in hand. "I don't understand that window," he said, shaking his finger towards it as he spoke. "Not at all. Why should Main want to get in and out by a window? He wasn't a stranger."

Hewitt began a most careful inspection of the whole surface of floor, ceiling, walls and furniture of the sitting-room. At the fireplace he stooped and lifted with great care a few sheets of charred paper from the grate. These he put on the window-ledge. "Will you just bring over that little screen," he asked, "to keep the draught from this burnt paper? Thank you. It looks like letter paper, and thick letter paper, since the ashes are very little broken. The weather has been fine, and there has been no fire in that grate for a long time. These papers have been carefully burned with a match or a candle."

"Ah! perhaps the letters poor young Rewse was writing in the morning. But what can they tell us?"

"Perhaps nothing—perhaps a great deal." Hewitt was examining the cinders keenly, holding the surface sideways to the light. "Come," he said, "see if I can guess Rewse's address in London. 17 Mountjoy Gardens, Hampstead. Is that it?"

"Yes. Is it there? Can you read it? Show me." Mr. Bowyer hurried across the room, eager and excited.

"You can sometimes read words on charred paper," Hewitt replied, "as you may have noticed. This has curled and crinkled rather too much in the burning, but it is plainly notepaper with an embossed heading, which stands out rather clearly. He has evidently brought some notepaper with him from home in his trunk. See, you can just see the ink lines crossing out the address; but there's little else. At the beginning of the letter there is 'My d—' then a gap, and then the last stroke of 'M' and the rest of the word 'mother.' 'My dear Mother,' or 'My dearest Mother' evidently. Something follows too in the same line, but that is unreadable. 'My dear Mother and Sister' perhaps. After that there is nothing recognisable. The first letter looks rather like 'W,' but even that is indistinct. It seems to be a longish letter—several sheets, but they are stuck together in the charring. Perhaps more than one letter."

"The thing is plain," Mr. Bowyer said. "The poor lad was writing home, and perhaps to other places, and Main, after his crime, burned the letters, because they would have stultified his own with the lying tale about small-pox."

Hewitt said nothing, but resumed his general search. He passed his hand rapidly over every inch of the surface of everything in the room. Then he entered the bedroom and began an inspection of the same sort there. There were two beds, one at each end of the room, and each inch of each piece of bed linen passed rapidly under his sharp eye. After the bedroom he betook himself to the little bath-room, and then to the scullery. Finally he went outside and examined every board of a close fence that stood a few feet from the sitting-room window, and the brick-paved path lying between.

When it was all over he returned to Mr. Bowyer. "Here is a strange thing," he said. "The shot passed clean through Rewse's body, striking no bones, and meeting no solid resistance. It was a good-sized bullet, as Dr. O'Reilly testifies, and therefore must have had a large charge of powder behind it in the cartridge. After emerging from Rewse's back it must have struck something else in this confined place. Yet on nowhere—ceiling, floor, wall nor furniture—can I find the mark of a bullet nor the bullet itself."

"The bullet itself Main might easily have got rid of."

"Yes, but not the mark. Indeed, the bullet would scarcely be easy to get at if it had struck anything I have seen about here; it would have buried itself. Just look round now. Where could a bullet strike in this place without leaving its mark?"

Mr. Bowyer looked round. "Well, no," he said, "nowhere. Unless the window was open and it went out that way."

"Then it must have hit the fence or the brick paving between, and there is no sign of a bullet there," Hewitt replied. "Push the sash as high as you please, the shot couldn't have passed over the fence without hitting the window first. As to the bedroom windows, that's impossible. Mr. Shanahan and his friends would not only have heard the shot, they would have seen it—which they didn't."

"Then what's the meaning of it?"

"The meaning of it is simply this: either Rewse was shot somewhere else and his body brought here afterwards, or the article, whatever it was, that the bullet struck must have been taken away."

"Yes, of course. It's just another piece of evidence destroyed by Main, that's all. Every step we go we see the diabolical completeness of his plans. But now every piece of evidence missing only tells the more against him. The body alone condemns him past all redemption."

Hewitt was gazing about the room thoughtfully. "I think we'll have Mrs. Hurley over here," he said; "she should tell us if anything is missing. Constable, will you ask Mrs. Hurley to step over here?"

Mrs. Hurley came at once and was brought into the sitting-room. "Just look about you, Mrs. Hurley," Hewitt said, "in this room and everywhere else, and tell me if anything is missing that you can remember was here on the morning of the day you last saw Mr. Rewse."

She looked thoughtfully up and down the room. "Sure, sor," she said, "'tis all there as ord'nary." Her eyes rested on the mantelpiece and she added at once, "Except the clock, indade."

"Except the clock?"

"The clock ut is, sure. Ut stud on that same mantelpiece on that mornin' as ut always did."

"What sort of clock was it?"

"Just a plain round wan wid a metal case—an American clock they said ut was. But ut kept nigh as good time as me own."

"It did keep good time, you say?"

"Faith an' ut did, sor. Mine an' this ran together for weeks wid nivir a minute betune thim."

"Thank you, Mrs. Hurley, thank you; that will do," Hewitt exclaimed, with something of excitement in his voice. He turned to Mr. Bowyer. "We must find that clock," he said. "And there's the pistol; nothing has been seen of that. Come, help me search. Look for a loose board."

"But he'll have taken them away with him, probably."

"The pistol perhaps—althought that isn't likely. The clock, no. It's evidence, man, evidence!" Hewitt darted outside and walked hurriedly round the cottage, looking this way and that about the country adjacent.

Presently he returned. "No," he said, "I think it's more likely in the house." He stood for a moment and thought. Then he made for the fireplace and flung the fender across the floor. All round the hearthstone an open crack extended. "See there!" he exclaimed as he pointed to it. He took the tongs, and with one leg levered the stone up till he could seize it in his fingers. Then he dragged it out and pushed it across the linoleum that covered the floor. In the space beneath lay a large revolver and a common American round nickel-plated clock. "See here!" he cried, "see here!" and he rose and placed the articles on the mantel-piece. The glass before the clock-face was smashed to atoms, and there was a gaping rent in the face itself. For a few seconds Hewitt regarded it as it stood, and then he turned to Mr. Bowyer. "Mr. Bowyer," he said, "we have done Mr. Stanley Main a sad injustice. Poor young Rewse committed suicide. There is proof undeniable," and he pointed to the clock.

"Proof? How? Where? Nonsense, man. Pooh! Ridiculous! If Rewse committed suicide why should Main go to all that trouble and tell all those lies to prove that he died of small-pox? More even than that, what has he run away for?"

"I'll tell you, Mr. Bowyer, in a moment. But first as to this clock. Remember, Main set his watch by the Cullanin Town Hall clock, and Mrs. Hurley's clock agreed exactly. That we have proved ourselves to-day by my own watch. Mrs. Hurley's clock still agrees. This clock was always kept in time with Mrs. Hurley's. Main returned at two exactly. Look at the time by that clock—the time when the bullet crashed into and stopped it."

The time was three minutes to one.

Hewitt took the clock, unscrewed the winder and quickly stripped off the back, exposing the works. "See," he said, "the bullet is lodged firmly among the wheels, and has been torn into snags and strips by the impact. The wheels themselves are ruined altogether. The central axle which carries the hands is bent. See there! Neither hand will move in the slightest. That bullet struck the axle and fixed those hands immovably at the moment of time when Algernon Rewse died. Look at the mainspring. It is less than half rim out. Proof that the clock was going when the shot struck it. Main left Rowse alive and well at half-past nine. He did not return till two—when Rewse had been dead more than an hour."

"But then, hang it all! How about the lies, and the false certificate, and the bolting?"

"Let me tell you the whole tale, Mr. Bowyer, as I conjecture it to have been. Poor young Rewse was, as you told me, in a bad state of health—thoroughly run down, I think you said. You said something of his engagement and the death of the lady. This pointed clearly to a nervous—a mental upset. Very well. He broods, and so forth. He must go away and find change of scene and occupation. His intimate friend Main brings him here. The holiday has its good effect perhaps, at first, but after a while it gets monotonous, and brooding sets in again. I do not know whether or not you happen to know it, but it is a fact that four-fifths of all persons suffering from melancholia have suicidal tendencies. This may never have been suspected by Main, who otherwise might not have left him so long alone. At any rate he is left alone, and he takes the opportunity. He writes a note to Main and a long letter to his mother—an awful, heartbreaking letter, with a terrible picture of the mental agony wherein he was to die—perhaps with a tincture of religious mania in it, and prophesying merited hell for himself in the hereafter. This done, he simply stands up from this table, at which he has been writing, and with his back to the fire-place shoots himself. There he lies till Main returns an hour later. Main finds the door shut and nobody answers his knock. He goes round to the sitting-room window, looks through, and perhaps he sees the body.

"Anyway he pushes back the catch with his knife, opens the window and gets in, and then he sees. He is completely knocked out of time. The thing is terrible. What shall he—what can he do? Poor Rewse's mother and sister dote on him, and his mother is an invalid—heart disease. To let her see that awful letter would be to kill her. He burns the letter, also the note to himself. Then an idea strikes him. Even without the letter the news of her boy's suicide will probably kill the poor old lady. Can she be prevented hearing of it? Of his death she must know—that's inevitable. But as to the manner? Would it not be possible to concoct some kind lie? And then the opportunities of the situation occur to him. Nobody but himself knows of it. He is a medical man, fully qualified, and empowered to give certificates of death.

"More, there is an epidemic of small-pox in the neighbourhood. What easier, with a little management, than to call the death one by small-pox? Nobody would be anxious to examine too closely the corpse of a smallpox patient. He decides that he will do it. He writes the letter to Mrs. Rewse announcing that her son has the disease, and he forbids Mrs. Hurley to come near the place for fear of infection. He cleans the floor—it is linoleum here, you see, and the stains were fresh—burns the clothes, cleans and stops the wound. At every turn his medical knowledge is of use. He puts the smashed clock and the pistol out of sight under the hearth. In a word he carries out the whole thing rather cleverly, and a terrible few days he must have passed. It never strikes him that he has dug a frightful pit for his own feet. You are suspicious, and you come across. In a perhaps rather peremptory manner You tell him how suspicious his conduct has been. And then a sense of his terrible position comes upon him like a thunderclap. He sees it all. He has deliberately of his own motion destroyed every evidence of the suicide. There is no evidence in the world that Rewse did not die a natural death, except the body, and that you are going to dig up. He sees now (you remind him of it in fact) that he is the one man alive who can profit by Rewse's death. And there is the shot body, and there is the false death certificate, and there are the lying letters, and the tales to the neighbours and everything. He has himself destroyed everything that proves suicide. All that remains points to a foul murder and to him as the murderer. Can you wonder at his complete breakdown and his flight? What else in the world could the poor fellow do?"

"Well well—yes, yes," Mr. Bowyer replied thoughtfully, "it seems very plausible of course. But still, look at probabilities, my dear sir, look at probabilities."

"No, but look at possibilities. There is that clock. Get over it if you can. Was there ever a more insurmountable alibi? Could Main possibly be here shooting Rewse and half way between here and Cullanin at the same time? Remember, Mrs. Hurley saw him come back at two, and she had been watching for an hour, and could see more than half a mile up the road."

"Well, yes, I suppose you're right. And what must we do now?"

"Bring Main back. I think we should advertise to begin with. Say, 'Rewse is proved to have died over an hour before you came. All safe. Your evidence is wanted,' or something of that sort. And we must set the telegraph going. The police already are looking for him, no doubt. Meanwhile I will look here for a clue myself."

The advertisement was successful in two days. Indeed Main afterwards said that he was at the time, once the first terror was over, in doubt whether or not it would be best to go back and face the thing out, trusting to his innocence. He could not venture home for money, nor to his bank, for fear of the police. He chanced, upon the advertisement as he searched the paper for news of the case, and that decided him. His explanation of the matter was precisely as Hewitt had expected. His only thought till Mr. Bowyer first arrived at the cottage had been to smother the real facts and to spare the feelings of Mrs. Rewse and her daughter, and it was not till that gentleman put them so plainly before him that he in the least realised the dangers of his position. That his fears for Mrs. Rewse were only too well grounded was proved by events, for the poor old lady only survived her son by a month.

These events took place some little while ago, as may be gathered from the fact that Miss Rewse has now been Mrs. Stanley Main for nearly three years.

VI. — THE CASE OF THE WARD LANE TABERNACLE

I

Among the few personal friendships that Martin Hewitt has allowed himself to make there is one for an eccentric but very excellent old lady named Mrs. Mallett. She must be more than seventy now, but she is of robust and active, not to say masculine, habits, and her relations with Hewitt are irregular and curious. He may not see her for many weeks, perhaps for months, until one day she will appear in the office, push Kerrett (who knows better than to attempt to stop her) into the inner room, and salute Hewitt with a shake of the hand and a savage glare of the eye which would appall a stranger, but which is quite amiably meant. As for myself, it was long ere I could find any resource but instant retreat before her gaze, though we are on terms of moderate toleration now.

After her first glare she sits in the chair by the window and directs her glance at Hewitt's small gas grill and kettle in the fireplace—a glance which Hewitt, with all expedition, translates into tea. Slightly mollified by the tea, Mrs. Mallett condescends to remark in tones of tragic truculence, on passing matters of conventional interest—the weather, the influenza, her own health, Hewitt's health, and so forth, any reply of Hewitt's being commonly received with either disregard or contempt.

In half an hour's time or so she leaves the office with a stern command to Hewitt to attend at her house and drink tea on a day and at a time named—a command which Hewitt obediently fulfills, when he passes through a similarly exhilarating experience in Mrs. Mallett's back drawing-room at her little freehold house in Fulham. Altogether Mrs. Mallett, to a stranger, is a singularly uninviting personality, and indeed, except Hewitt, who has learnt to appreciate her hidden good qualities, I doubt if she has a friend in the world. Her studiously concealed charities are a matter of as much amusement as gratification to Hewitt, who naturally, in the course of his peculiar profession, comes across many sad examples of poverty and suffering, commonly among the decent sort, who hide their troubles from strangers' eyes and suffer in secret. When such a case is in his mind it is Hewitt's practice to inform Mrs. Mallett of it at one of the tea ceremonies. Mrs. Mallett receives the story with snorts of incredulity and scorn but takes care, while expressing the most callous disregard and contempt of the troubles of the sufferers, to ascertain casually their names and addresses; twenty-four hours after which Hewitt need only make a visit to find their difficulties in some mysterious way alleviated.

Mrs. Mallett never had any children, and was early left a widow. Her appearance, for some reason or another, commonly leads strangers to believe her an old maid. She lives in her little detached house with its square piece of ground, attended by a house-keeper older than herself and one maid-servant. She lost her only sister by death soon after the events I am about to set down, and now has, I believe, no relations in the world. It was also soon after these events that her present housekeeper first came to her in place of an older and very deaf woman, quite useless, who had been with her before. I believe she is moderately rich, and that one or two charities will benefit considerably at her death; also I should be far from astonished to find Hewitt's own name in her will, though this is no more than idle conjecture. The one possession to which she clings with all her soul—her one pride and treasure—is her great-uncle Joseph's snuff-box, the lid of which she steadfastly believes to be made of a piece of Noah's original ark discovered on the top of Mount Ararat by some intrepid explorer of vague identity about a hundred years ago. This is her one weakness, and woe to the unhappy creature who dares hint a suggestion that possibly the wood of the ark rotted away to nothing a few thousand years before her great-uncle Joseph ever took snuff. I believe he would be bodily assaulted. The box is brought for Hewitt's admiration at every tea ceremony at Fulham, when Hewitt handles it reverently and expresses as much astonishment and interest as if he had never seen or heard of it before. It is on these occasions only that Mrs. Mallett's customary stiffness relaxes. The sides of the box are of cedar of Lebanon, she explains (which very possibly they are), and the gold mountings were worked up from spade guineas (which one can believe without undue strain on the reason). And it is usually these times, when the old lady softens under the combined influence of tea and uncle Joseph's snuff-box, that Hewitt seizes to lead up to his hint of some starving governess or distressed clerk, with the full confidence that the more savagely the story is received the better will the poor people be treated as soon as he turns his back.

It was her jealous care of uncle Joseph's snuff-box that first brought Mrs. Mallett into contact with Martin Hewitt, and the occasion, though not perhaps testing his acuteness to the extent that some did, was nevertheless one of the most curious and fantastic on which he has ever been engaged She was then some ten or twelve years younger than she is now, but Hewitt assures me she looked exactly the same; that is to say, she was harsh, angular, and seemed little more than fifty years of age. It was before the time of Kerrett, and another youth occupied the outer office. Hewitt sat late one afternoon with his door ajar when he heard a stranger enter the outer office, and a voice, which he afterwards knew well as Mrs. Mallett's, ask "Is Mr. Martin Hewitt in?"

"Yes, ma'am, I think so. If you will write your name and—"

"Is he in there?" And with three strides Mrs. Mallett was at the inner door and stood before Hewitt himself, while the routed office-lad stared helplessly in the rear.

"Mr. Hewitt," Mrs. Mallet said, "I have come to put an affair into your hands, which I shall require to be attended to at once."

Hewitt was surprised, but he bowed politely, and said, with some suspicion of a hint in his tone, "Yes—I rather supposed you were in a hurry."

She glanced quickly in Hewitt's face and went on: "I am not accustomed to needless ceremony, Mr. Hewitt. My name is Mallett—Mrs. Mallett—and here is my card. I have come to consult you on a matter of great annoyance and some danger to myself. The fact is I am being watched and followed by a number of persons."

Hewitt's gaze was steadfast, but he reflected that possibly this curious woman was a lunatic, the delusion of being watched and followed by unknown people being perhaps the most common of all; also it was no unusual thing to have a lunatic visit the office with just such a complaint. So he only said soothingly, "Indeed? That must be very annoying."

"Yes, yes, the annoyance is bad enough perhaps," she answered shortly, "but I am chiefly concerned about my great-uncle Joseph's snuff-box."

This utterance sounded a trifle more insane than the other, so Hewitt answered, a little more soothingly still: "Ah, of course. A very important thing, the snuff-box, no doubt."

"It is, Mr. Hewitt—it is important, as I think you will admit when you have seen it. Here it is," and she produced from a small handbag the article that Hewitt was destined so often again to see and affect an interest in. "You may be incredulous, Mr. Hewitt, but it is nevertheless a fact that the lid of this snuff-box is made of the wood of the original ark that rested on Mount Ararat."

She handed the box to Hewitt, who murmured, "Indeed! Very interesting—very wonderful, really," and returned it to the lady immediately.

"That, Mr. Hewitt, was the property of my great-uncle, Joseph Simpson, who once had the honour of shaking hands with his late Majesty King George the Fourth. The box was presented to my uncle by—," and then Mrs. Mallett plunged into the whole history and adventures of the box, in the formula wherewith Hewitt subsequently became so well acquainted, and which need not be here set out in detail. When the box had been properly honoured Mrs. Mallett proceeded with her business.

"I am convinced, Mr. Hewitt," she said, "that systematic attempts are being made to rob me of this snuff-box. I am not a nervous or weak-minded woman, or perhaps I might have sought your assistance before. The watching and following of myself I might have disregarded, but when it comes to burglary I think it is time to do something."

"Certainly," Hewitt agreed.

"Well, I have been pestered with demands for the box for some time past. I have here some of the letters which I have received, and I am sure I know at whose instigation they were sent." She placed on the table a handful of papers of various sizes, which Hewitt examined one after another. They were mostly in the same handwriting, and all were unsigned. Every one was couched in a fanatically toned imitation of scriptural diction, and all sorts of threats were expressed with many emphatic underlinings. The spelling was not of the best, the writing was mostly uncouth, and the grammar was in ill shape in many places, the "thous" and "thees" and their accompanying verbs falling over each other disastrously. The purport of the messages was rather vaguely expressed, but all seemed to make a demand for the restoration of some article held in extreme veneration. This was alluded to in many figurative ways as the "token of life," the "seal of the woman," and so forth, and sometimes Mrs. Mallett was requested to restore it to the "ark of the covenant." One of the least vague of these singular documents ran thus:— "Thou of no faith put the bond of the woman clothed with the sun on the stoan sete in thy back garden this night or thy blood beest on your own hed. Give it back to us the five righteous only in this citty, give us that what saves the faithful when the erth is swalloed up." Hewitt read over these fantastic missives one by one till he began to suspect that his client, mad or not, certainly corresponded with mad Quakers. Then he said, "Yes, Mrs. Mallett, these are most extraordinary letters. Are there any more of them?"

"Bless the man, yes, there were a lot that I burnt. All the same crack-brained sort of thing."

"They are mostly in one handwriting," Hewitt said, "though some are in another. But I confess I don't see any very direct reference to the snuff-box."

"Oh, but it's the only thing they can mean," Mrs. Mallett replied with great positiveness. "Why, he wanted me to sell it him; and last night my house was broken into in my absence and everything ransacked and turned over, but not a thing was taken. Why? Because I had the box with me at my sister's; and this is the only sacred relic in my possession. And what saved the faithful when the world was swallowed up? Why, the ark of course." The old lady's manner was odd, but notwithstanding the bizarre and disjointed character of her complaint Hewitt had now had time to observe that she had none of the unmistakable signs of the lunatic. Her eye was steady and clear, and she had none of the restless habits of the mentally deranged. Even at that time Hewitt had met with curious adventures enough to teach him not to be astonished at a new one, and now he set himself seriously to get at his client's case in full order and completeness.

"Come, Mrs. Mallett," he said, "I am a stranger, and I can never understand your case till I have it, not as it presents itself to your mind, in the order of importance of events, but in the exact order in which they happened. You had a great-uncle, I understand, living in the early part of the century, who left you at his death the snuff-box which you value so highly. Now you suspect that somebody is attempting to extort or steal it from you. Tell me as clearly and simply as you can whom you suspect and the whole story of the attempts."

"That's just what I'm coming to," the old lady answered, rather pettishly. "My uncle Joseph had an old housekeeper, who of course knew all about the snuff-box, and it is her son Reuben Penner who is trying to get it from me. The old woman was half crazy with one extraordinary religious superstition and another, and her son seems to be just the same. My great-uncle was a man of strong common-sense and a churchman (though he did think he could write plays), and if it hadn't been for his restraint I believe—that is I have been told—Mrs. Penner would have gone clean demented with religious mania. Well, she died in course of time, and my great-uncle died some time after, leaving me the most important thing in his possession (I allude to the snuff-box of course), a good bit of property, and a tin box full of his worthless manuscript. I became a widow at twenty-six, and since then I have lived very quietly in my present house in Fulham.

"A couple of years ago I received a visit from Reuben Penner. I didn't recognise him, which wasn't wonderful, since I hadn't seen him for thirty years or more. He is well over fifty now, a large heavy-faced man with uncommonly wild eyes for a greengrocer—which is what he is, though he dresses very well, considering. He was quite respectful at first, and very awkward in his manner. He took a little time to get his courage, and then he began questioning me about my religious feelings. Well, Mr. Hewitt, I am not the sort of person to stand a lecture from a junior and an inferior, whatever my religious opinions may be, and I pretty soon made him realise it. But somehow he persevered. He wanted to know if I would go to some place of worship that he called his 'Tabernacle.' I asked him who was the pastor. He said himself. I asked him how many members of the congregation there were, and (the man was as solemn as an owl. I assure you, Mr. Hewitt) he actually said five! I kept my countenance and asked why such a small number couldn't attend church, or at any rate attach itself to some decent Dissenting chapel. And then the man burst out; mad—mad as a hatter. He was as incoherent as such people usually are, but as far as I could make out he talked, among a lot of other things, of some imaginary woman—a woman standing on the moon and driven into a wilderness on the wings of an eagle. The man was so madly possessed of his fancies that I assure you for a while he almost ceased to look ridiculous. He was so earnest in his rant. But I soon cut him short. It's best to be severe with these people—it's the only chance of bringing them to their senses. 'Reuben Penner,' I said, 'shut up! Your mother was a very decent person in her way, I believe, but she was half a lunatic with her superstitious notions, and you're a bigger fool than she was. Imagine a grown man, and of your age, coming and asking me, of all people in the world, to leave my church and make another fool in a congregation of five, with you to rave at me about women in the moon! Go away and look after your greengrocery, and go to church or chapel like a sensible man. Go away and don't play the fool any longer; I won't hear another word!'

"When I talk like this I am usually attended to, and in this case Penner went away with scarcely another word. I saw nothing of him for about a month or six weeks and then he came and spoke to me as I was cutting roses in my front garden. This time he talked—to begin with, at least—more sensibly. 'Mrs. Mallett,' he said, 'you have in your keeping a very sacred relic.'

"'I have,' I said, 'left me by my great-uncle Joseph. And what then?'

"'Well'—he hummed and hawed a little—'I wanted to ask if you might be disposed to part with it.'

"'What?' I said, dropping my scissors—'sell it?'

"'Well, yes,' he answered, putting on as bold a face as he could.

"The notion of selling my uncle Joseph's snuff-box in any possible circumstances almost made me speechless. 'What!' I repeated. 'Sell it?—sell it? It would be a sinful sacrilege!'

"His face quite brightened when I said this, and he replied, 'Yes, of course it would; I think so myself, ma'am; but I fancied you thought otherwise. In that case, ma'am, not being a believer yourself, I'm sure you would consider it a graceful and a pious act to present it to my little Tabernacle, where it would be properly valued. And it having been my mother's property—'

"He got no further. I am not a woman to be trifled with, Mr. Hewitt, and I believe I beat him out of the garden with my basket. I was so infuriated I can scarcely remember what I did. The suggestion that I should sell my uncle Joseph's snuff-box to a greengrocer was bad enough; the request that I should actually give it to his 'Tabernacle' was infinitely worse. But to claim that it had belonged to his mother—well I don't know how it strikes you, Mr. Hewitt, but to me it seemed the last insult possible."

"Shocking, shocking, of course," Hewitt said, since she seemed to expect a reply. "And he called you an unbeliever, too. But what happened after that?"

"After that he took care not to bother me personally again; but these wretched anonymous demands came in, with all sorts of darkly hinted threats as to the sin I was committing in keeping my own property. They didn't trouble me much. I put 'em in the fire as fast as they came, until I began to find I was being watched and followed, and then I kept them."

"Very sensible," Hewitt observed, "very sensible indeed to do that. But tell me as to these papers. Those you have here are nearly all in one handwriting, but some, as I have already said, are in another. Now before all this business, did you ever see Reuben Penner's handwriting?"

"No, never."

"Then you are not by any means sure that he has written any of these things?"

"But then who else could?"

"That of course is a thing to be found out. At present, at any rate, we know this: that if Penner has anything to do with these letters he is not alone, because of the second handwriting. Also we must not bind ourselves past other conviction that he wrote any one of them. By the way, I am assuming that they all arrived by post?"

"Yes, they did."

"But the envelopes are not here. Have you kept any of them?"

"I hardly know; there may be some at home. Is it important?"

"It may be; but those I can see at another time. Please go on."

"These things continued to arrive, as I have said, and I continued to burn them till I began to find myself watched and followed, and then I kept them. That was two or three months ago. It is a most unpleasant sensation, that of feeling that some unknown person is dogging your footsteps from corner to corner and observing all your movements for a purpose you are doubtful of. Once or twice I turned suddenly back, but I never could catch the creatures, of whom I am sure Penner was one."

"You saw these people, of course?"

"Well, yes, in a way—with the corner of my eye, you know. But it was mostly in the evening. It was a woman once, but several times I feel certain it was Penner. And once I saw a man come into my garden at the back in the night, and I feel quite sure that was Penner."

"Was that after you had this request to put the article demanded on the stone seat in the garden?"

"The same night. I sat up and watched from the bath-room window, expecting someone would come. It was a dark night, and the trees made it darker, but I could plainly see someone come quietly over the wall and go up to the seat."

"Could you distinguish his face?"

"No, it was too dark. But I feel sure it was Penner."

"Has Penner any decided peculiarity of form or gait?"

"No, he's just a big common sort of man. But I tell you I feel certain it was Penner."

"For any particular reason?"

"No, perhaps not. But who else could it have been? No, I'm very sure it must have been Penner."

Hewitt repressed a smile and went on. "Just so," he said. "And what happened then?"

"He went up to the seat, as I said, and looked at it, passing his hand over the top. Then I called out to him. I said if I found him on my premises again by day or night I'd give him in charge of the police. I assure you he got over the wall the second time a good deal quicker than the first. And then I went to bed, though I got a shocking cold in the head sitting at that open bath-room window. Nobody came about the place after that till last night. A few days ago my only sister was taken ill. I saw her each day, and she got worse. Yesterday she was so bad that I wouldn't leave her. I sent home for some things and stopped in her house for the night. To-day I got an urgent message to come home, and when I went I found that an entrance had been made by a kitchen window and the whole house had been ransacked, but not a thing was missing."

"Were drawers and boxes opened?"

"Everywhere. Most seemed to have been opened with keys, but some were broken. The place was turned upside down, but, as I said before, not a thing was missing. A very old woman, very deaf, who used to be my housekeeper, but who does nothing now, was in the house, and so was my general servant. They slept in rooms at the top and were not disturbed. Of course the old woman is too deaf to have heard anything, and the maid is a very heavy sleeper. The girl was very frightened, but I pacified her before I came away. As it happened, I took the snuff-box with me. I had got very suspicious of late, of course, and something seemed to suggest that I had better so I took it. It's pretty strong evidence that they have been watching me closely, isn't it, that they should break in the very first night I left the place?"

"And are you quite sure that nothing has been taken?"

"Quite certain. I have spent a long time in a very careful search."

"And you want me, I presume, to find out definitely who these people are, and get such evidence as may ensure their being punished?"

"That is the case. Of course I know Reuben Penner is the moving spirit—I'm quite certain of that. But still I can see plainly enough that as yet there's no legal evidence of it. Mind, I'm not afraid of him—not a bit. That is not my character. I'm not afraid of all the madmen in England; but I'm not going to have them steal my property—this snuff-box especially."

"Precisely. I hope you have left the disturbance in your house exactly as you found it?"

"Oh, of course, and I have given strict orders that nothing is to be touched. To-morrow morning I should like you to come and look at it."

"I must look at it, certainly," Hewitt said, "but I would rather go at once."

"Pooh—nonsense!" Mrs. Mallett answered, with the airy obstinacy that Hewitt afterwards knew so well. "I'm not going home again now to spend an hour or two more. My sister will want to know what has become of me, and she mustn't suspect that anything is wrong, or it may do all sorts of harm. The place will keep till the morning, and I have the snuff-box safe with me. You have my card, Mr. Hewitt, haven't you? Very well. Can you be at my house to-morrow morning at half-past ten? I will be there, and you can see all you want by daylight. We'll consider that settled. Good-day." Hewitt saw her to his office door and waited till she had half descended the stairs. Then he made for a staircase window which gave a view of the street. The evening was coming on murky and foggy, and the street lights were blotchy and vague. Outside a four-wheeled cab stood, and the driver eagerly watched the front door. When Mrs. Mallett emerged he instantly began to descend from the box with the quick invitation, "Cab, mum, cab?"

He seemed very eager for his fare, and though Mrs. Mallett hesitated a second she eventually entered the cab. He drove off, and Hewitt tried in vain to catch a glimpse of the number of the cab behind. It was always a habit of his to note all such identifying marks throughout a case, whether they seemed important at the time or not, and he has often had occasion to be pleased with the outcome. Now, however, the light was too bad. No sooner had the cab started than a man emerged from a narrow passage opposite, and followed. He was a large, rather awkward, heavy-faced man of middle age, and had the appearance of a respectable artisan or small tradesman in his best clothes. Hewitt hurried downstairs and followed the direction the cab and the man had taken, toward the Strand. But the cab by this time was swallowed up in the Strand traffic, and the heavy-faced man had also disappeared. Hewitt returned to his office a little disappointed, for the man seemed rather closely to answer Mrs. Mallett's description of Reuben Penner.

II

Punctually at half-past ten the next morning Hewitt was at Mrs. Mallett's house at Fulham. It was a pretty little house, standing back from the road in a generous patch of garden, and had evidently stood there when Fulham was an outlying village. Hewitt entered the gate, and made his way to the front door, where two young females, evidently servants, stood. They were in a very disturbed state, and when he asked for Mrs. Mallett, assured him that nobody knew where she was, and that she had not been seen since the previous afternoon.

"But," said Hewitt, "she was to stay at her sister's last night, I believe."

"Yes, sir," answered the more distressed of the two girls—she in a cap—"but she hasn't been seen there. This is her sister's servant, and she's been sent over to know where she is, and why she hasn't been there." This the other girl—in bonnet and shawl—corroborated. Nothing had been seen of Mrs. Mallett at her sister's since she had received the message the day before to the effect that the house had been broken into.

"And I'm so frightened," the other girl said, whimperingly. "They've been in the place again last night."

"Who have?"

"The robbers. When I came in this morning—"

"But didn't you sleep here?"

"I—I ought to ha' done sir, but—but after Mrs. Mallett went yesterday I got so frightened I went home at ten." And the girl showed signs of tears, which she had apparently been already indulging in.

"And what about the old woman—the deaf woman; where was she?"

"She was in the house, sir. There was nowhere else for her to go, and she was deaf and didn't know anything about what happened the night before, and confined to her room, and—and so I didn't tell her."

"I see," Hewitt said with a slight smile. "You left her here. She didn't see or hear anything, did she?"

"No sir; she can't hear, and she didn't see nothing."

"And how do you know thieves have been in the house?"

"Everythink's tumbled about worse than ever, sir, and all different from what it was yesterday; and there's a box o' papers in the attic broke open, and all sorts o' things."

"Have you spoken to the police?"

"No, sir; I'm that frightened I don't know what to do. And missis was going to see a gentleman about it yesterday, and—"

"Very well, I am that gentleman—Mr. Martin Hewitt. I have come down now to meet her by appointment. Did she say she was going anywhere else as well as to my office and to her sister's?"

"No, sir. And she—she's got the snuff-box with her and all." This latter circumstance seemed largely to augment the girl's terrors for her mistress's safety.

"Very well," Hewitt said, "I think I'd better just look over the house now, and then consider what has become of Mrs. Mallett—if she isn't heard of in the meantime." The girl found a great relief in Hewitt's presence in the house, the deaf old house-keeper, who seldom spoke and never heard, being, as she said, "worse than nobody."

"Have you been in all the rooms?" Hewitt asked.

"No, sir; I was afraid. When I came in I went straight upstairs to my room, and as I was coming away I see the things upset in the other attic. I went into Mrs. Perks' room, next to mine (she's the deaf old woman), and she was there all right, but couldn't hear anything. Then I came down and only just peeped into two of the rooms and saw the state they were in, and then I came out into the garden, and presently this young woman came with the message from Mrs. Rudd."

"Very well, we'll look at the rooms now," Hewitt said, and they proceeded to do so. All were in a state of intense confusion. Drawers, taken from chests and bureaux, littered about the floor, with their contents scattered about them. Carpets and rugs had been turned up and flung into corners, even pictures on the walls had been disturbed, and while some hung awry others rested on the floor and on chairs. The things, however, appeared to have been fairly carefully handled, for nothing was damaged except one or two framed engravings, the brown paper on the backs of which had been cut round with a knife and the wooden slats shifted so as to leave the backs of the engravings bare. This, the girl told Hewitt, had not been done on the night of the first burglary; the other articles also had not on that occasion been so much disturbed as they now were.

Mrs. Mallett's bedroom was the first floor front. Here the confusion was, if possible, greater than in the other rooms. The bed had been completely unmade and the clothes thrown separately on the floor, and everything else was displaced. It was here indeed that the most noticeable features of the disturbance were observed, for on the side of the looking-glass hung a very long old-fashioned gold chain untouched, and on the dressing-table lay a purse with the money still in it. And on the looking-glass, stuck into the crack of the frame, was a half sheet of notepaper with this inscription scrawled in pencil:—

To Mr. Martin Hewitt.

Mrs. Mallett is alright and in frends hands. She will return soon alright, if you keep quiet. But if you folloe her or take any steps the conseqinses will be very serious.

This paper was not only curious in itself, and curious as being addressed to Hewitt, but it was plainly in the same handwriting as were the most of the anonymous letters which Mrs. Mallett had produced the day before in Hewitt's office. Hewitt studied it attentively for a few moments and then thrust it in his pocket and proceeded to inspect the rest of the rooms. All were the same—simply well-furnished rooms turned upside down. The top floor consisted of three comfortable attics, one used as a lumber-room and the others used respectively as bedrooms for the servant and the deaf old woman. None of these rooms appeared to have been entered, the girl said, on the first night, but now the lumber-room was almost as confused as the rooms downstairs. Two or three boxes were opened and their contents turned out. One of these was what is called a steel trunk—a small one—which had held old papers, the others were filled chiefly with old clothes.

The servant's room next this was quite undisturbed and untouched; and then Hewitt was admitted to the room of Mrs. Mallett's deaf old pensioner. The old woman sat propped up in her bed and looked with half-blind eyes at the peak in the bedclothes made by her bent knees. The servant screamed in her ear, but she neither moved nor spoke.

Hewitt laid his hand on her shoulder and said, in the slow and distinct tones he had found best for reaching the senses of deaf people, "I hope you are well. Did anything disturb you in the night?" But she only turned her head half toward him and mumbled peevishly, "I wish you'd bring my tea. You're late enough this morning." Nothing seemed likely to be got from her, and Hewitt asked the servant, "Is she altogether bedridden?"

"No," the girl answered; "leastways she needn't be. She stops in bed most of the time, but she can get up when she likes—I've seen her. But missis humours her and lets her do as she likes—and she gives plenty of trouble. I don't believe she's as deaf as she makes out."

"Indeed!" Hewitt answered. "Deafness is convenient sometimes, I know. Now I want you to stay here while I make some inquiries. Perhaps you'd better keep Mrs. Rudd's servant with you if you want company. I don't expect to be very long gone, and in any case it wouldn't do for her to go to her mistress and say that Mrs. Mallett is missing, or it might upset her seriously." Hewitt left the house and walked till he found a public-house where a post-office directory was kept. He took a glass of whisky and water, most of which he left on the counter, and borrowed the directory. He found "Greengrocers" in the "Trade" section and ran his finger down the column till he came on this address:—"Penner, Reuben, 8, Little Marsh Row, Hammersmith, W." Then he returned the directory and found the best cab he could to take him to Hammersmith.

Little Marsh Row was not a vastly prosperous sort of place, and the only shops were three—all small. Two were chandlers', and the third was a sort of semi-shed of the greengrocery and coal persuasion, with the name "Penner" on a board over the door.

The shutters were all up, though the door was open, and the only person visible was a very smudgy boy who was in the act of wheeling out a sack of coals. To the smudgy boy Hewitt applied himself. "I don't see Mr. Penner about," he said; "will he be back soon?"

The boy stared hard at Hewitt. "No," he said, "he won't. 'E's guv' up the shop. 'E paid 'is next week's rent this mornin' and retired."

"Oh!" Hewitt answered sharply. "Retired, has he? And what's become of the stock, eh! Where are the cabbages and potatoes?"

"'E told me to give 'em to the pore, an' I did. There's lots o' pore lives round 'ere. My mother's one, an' these 'ere coals is for 'er, an' I'm goin' to 'ave the trolley for myself."

"Dear me!" Hewitt answered, regarding the boy with amused interest. "You're a very business-like almoner. And what will the Tabernacle do without Mr. Penner?"

"I dunno," the boy answered, closing the door behind him. "I dunno nothin' about the Tabernacle—only where it is."

"Ah, and where is it? I might find him there, perhaps."

"Ward Lane—fust on left, second on right. It's a shop wot's bin shut up; next door to a stable-yard." And the smudgy boy started off with his trolley.

The Tabernacle was soon found. At some very remote period it had been an unlucky small shop, but now it was permanently shuttered, and the interior was lighted by holes cut in the upper panels of the shutters. Hewitt took a good look at the shuttered window and the door beside it and then entered the stable-yard at the side. To the left of the passage giving entrance to the yard there was a door, which plainly was another entrance to the house, and a still damp mud-mark on the step proved it to have been lately used. Hewitt rapped sharply at the door with his knuckles.

Presently a female voice from within could be heard speaking through the keyhole in a very loud whisper. "Who is it?" asked the voice.

Hewitt stooped to the keyhole and whispered back, "Is Mr. Penner here now?"

"No."

"Then I must come in and wait for him. Open the door." A bolt was pulled back and the door cautiously opened a few inches. Hewitt's foot was instantly in the jamb, and he forced the door back and entered. "Come," he said in a loud voice, "I've come to find out where Mr. Penner is, and to see whoever is in here." Immediately there was an assault of fists on the inside of a door at the end of the passage, and a loud voice said, "Do you hear? Whoever you are I'll give you five pounds if you'll bring Mr. Martin Hewitt here. His office is 25 Portsmouth Street, Strand. Or the same if you'll bring the police." And the voice was that of Mrs. Mallett.

Hewitt turned to the woman who had opened the door, and who now stood, much frightened, in the corner beside him. "Come," he said, "your keys, quick, and don't offer to stir, or I'll have you brought back and taken to the station." The woman gave him a bunch of keys without a word. Hewitt opened the door at the end of the passage, and once more Mrs. Mallett stood before him, prim and rigid as ever, except that her bonnet was sadly out of shape and her mantle was torn.

"Thank you, Mr. Hewitt," she said. "I thought you'd come, though where I am I know no more than Adam. Somebody shall smart severely for this. Why, and that woman—that woman," she pointed contemptuously at the woman in the corner, who was about two-thirds her height, "was going to search me—me! Why—" Mrs. Mallett, blazing with suddenly revived indignation, took a step forward and the woman vanished through the outer door.

"Come," Hewitt said, "no doubt you've been shamefully treated; but we must be quiet for a little. First I will make quite sure that nobody else is here, and then we'll get to your house." Nobody was there. The rooms were dreary and mostly empty. The front room, which was lighted by the holes in the shutters, had a rough reading-desk and a table, with half a dozen wooden chairs. "This," said Hewitt, "is no doubt the Tabernacle proper, and there is very little to see in it. Come back now, Mrs. Mallett, to your house, and we'll see if some explanation of these things is not possible. I hope your snuff-box is quite safe?"

Mrs. Mallett drew it from her pocket and exhibited it triumphantly. "I told them they should never get it," she said, "and they saw I meant it, and left off trying." As they emerged in the street she said: "The first thing, of course, is to bring the police into this place."

"No, I think we won't do that yet," Hewitt said. "In the first place the case is one of assault and detention, and your remedy is by summons or action; and then there are other things to speak of. We shall get a cab in the High Street, and you shall tell me what has happened to you."

Mrs. Mallett's story was simple. The cab in which she left Hewitt's office had travelled west, and was apparently making for the locality of her sister's house; but the evening was dark, the fog increased greatly, and she shut the windows and took no particular notice of the streets through which she was passing. Indeed with such a fog that would have been impossible. She had a sort of undefined notion that some of the streets were rather narrow and dirty, but she thought nothing of it, since all cabmen are given to selecting unexpected routes. After a time, however, the cab slowed, made a sharp turn, and pulled up. The door was opened, and "Here you are mum," said the cabby. She did not understand the sharp turn, and had a general feeling that the place could not be her sister's, but as she alighted she found she had stepped directly upon the threshold of a narrow door into which she was immediately pulled by two persons inside. This, she was sure, must have been the side-door in the stable-yard, through which Hewitt himself had lately obtained entrance to the Tabernacle.

Before she had recovered from her surprise the door was shut behind her. She struggled stoutly and screamed, but the place she was in was absolutely dark; she was taken by surprise, and she found resistance useless. They were men who held her, and the voice of the only one who spoke she did not know. He demanded in firm and distinct tones that the "sacred thing" should be given up, and that Mrs. Mallett should sign a paper agreeing to prosecute nobody before she was allowed to go. She however, as she asserted with her customary emphasis, was not the sort of woman to give in to that. She resolutely declined to do anything of the sort, and promised her captors, whoever they were, a full and legal return for their behaviour. Then she became conscious that a woman was somewhere present, and the man threatened that this woman should search her. This threat Mrs. Mallett met as boldly as the others. She should like to meet the woman who would dare attempt to search her, she said. She defied anybody to attempt it. As for her uncle Joseph's snuff-box, no matter where it was, it was where they would not be able to get it. That they should never have, but sooner or later they should have something very unpleasant for their attempts to steal it. This declaration had an immediate effect. They importuned her no more, and she was left in an inner room and the key was turned on her. There she sat, dozing occasionally, the whole night, her indomitable spirit remaining proof through all those doubtful hours of darkness. Once or twice she heard people enter and move about, and each time she called aloud to offer, as Hewitt had heard, a reward to anybody who should bring the police or communicate her situation to Hewitt. Day broke and still she waited, sleepless and unfed, till Hewitt at last arrived and released her.

On Mrs. Mallett's arrival at her house Mrs. Rudd's servant was at once despatched with reassuring news and Hewitt once more addressed himself to the question of the burglars. "First, Mrs. Mallett," he said, "did you ever conceal anything—anything at all mind—in the frame of an engraving?"

"No, never."

"Were any of your engravings framed before you had them?"

"Not one that I can remember. They were mostly uncle Joseph's, and he kept them with a lot of others in drawers. He was rather a collector, you know."

"Very well. Now come up to the attic. Something has been opened there that was not touched at the first attempt."

"See now," said Hewitt, when the attic was reached, "here is a box full of papers. Do you know everything that was in it?"

"No, I don't," Mrs. Mallett replied. "There were a lot of my uncle's manuscript plays. Here you see 'The Dead Bridegroom, or the Drum of Fortune,' and so on; and there were a lot of autographs. I took no interest in them, although some were rather valuable, I believe."

"Now bring your recollection to bear as strongly as you can," Hewitt said. "Do you ever remember seeing in this box a paper bearing nothing whatever upon it but a wax seal?"

"Oh yes, I remember that well enough. I've noticed it each time I've turned the box over—which is very seldom. It was a plain slip of vellum paper with a red seal, cracked and rather worn—some celebrated person's seal, I suppose. What about it?" Hewitt was turning the papers over one at a time. "It doesn't seem to be here now," he said. "Do you see it?"

"No," Mrs. Mallett returned, examining the papers herself, "it isn't. It appears to be the only thing missing. But why should they take it?"

"I think we are at the bottom of all this mystery now," Hewitt answered quietly. "It is the Seal of the Woman."

"The what? I don't understand. The fact is, Mrs. Mallett, that these people have never wanted your uncle Joseph's snuff-box at all, but that seal."

"Not wanted the snuff-box? Nonsense! Why, didn't I tell you Penner asked for it—wanted to buy it?"

"Yes, you did, but so far as I can remember you never spoke of a single instance of Penner mentioning the snuff-box by name. He spoke of a sacred relic, and you, of course, very naturally assumed he spoke of the box. None of the anonymous letters mentioned the box, you know, and once or twice they actually did mention a seal, though usually the thing was spoken of in a roundabout and figurative way. All along, these people—Reuben Penner and the others—have been after the seal, and you have been defending the snuff-box."

"But why the seal?"

"Did you never hear of Joanna Southcott?"

"Oh yes, of course; she was an ignorant visionary who set up as prophetess eighty or ninety years ago or more."

"Joanna Southcott gave herself out as a prophetess in 1790. She was to be the mother of the Messiah, she said, and she was the woman driven into the wilderness, as foretold in the twelfth chapter of the Book of Revelation. She died at the end of 1814, when her followers numbered more than 100,000, all fanatic believers. She had made rather a good thing in her lifetime by the sale of seals, each of which was to secure the eternal salvation of the holder. At her death, of course, many of the believers fell away, but others held on as faithfully as ever, asserting that 'the holy Joanna' would rise again and fulfil all the prophecies. These poor people dwindled in numbers gradually, and although they attempted to bring up their children in their own faith, the whole belief has been practically extinct for years now. You will remember that you told me of Penner's mother being a superstitious fanatic of some sort, and that your uncle Joseph possessed her extravagances. The thing seems pretty plain now. Your uncle Joseph possessed himself of Joanna Southcott's seal by way of removing from poor old Mrs. Penner an object of a sort of idolatry, and kept it as a curiosity. Reuben Penner grew up strong in his mother's delusions, and to him and the few believers he had gathered round him at his Tabernacle, the seal was an object worth risking anything to get.

"First he tried to convert you to his belief. Then he tried to buy it; after that, he and his friends tried anonymous letters, and at last, grown desperate, they resorted to watching you, burglary and kidnapping. Their first night's raid was unsuccessful, so last night they tried kidnapping you by the aid of a cabman. When they had got you, and you had at last given them to understand that it was your uncle Joseph's snuff-box you were defending, they tried the house again, and this time were successful. I guessed they had succeeded then, from a simple circumstance. They had begun to cut out the backs of framed engravings for purposes of search, but only some of the engravings were so treated. That meant either that the article wanted was found behind one of them, or that the intruders broke off in their picture-examination to search somewhere else, and were then successful, and so under no necessity of opening the other engravings. You assured me that nothing could have been concealed in any of the engravings, so I at once assumed that they had found what they were after in the only place wherein they had not searched the night before—the attic—and probably among the papers in the trunk."

"But then if they found it there why didn't they return and let me go?"

"Because you would have found where they had brought you. They probably intended to keep you there till the dark of the next evening, and then take you away in a cab again and leave you some distance off. To prevent my following and possibly finding you they left here on your looking-glass this note" (Hewitt produced it) "threatening all sorts of vague consequences if you were not left to them. They knew you had come to me, of course, having followed you to my office. And now Penner feels himself anything but safe. He has relinquished his greengrocery and dispensed his stock in charity, and probably, having got the seal he has taken himself off. Not so much perhaps from fear of punishment as for fear the seal may be taken from him, and with it the salvation his odd belief teaches him it will confer."

Mrs. Mallett sat silently for a little while and then said in a rather softened voice, "Mr. Hewitt, I am not what is called a woman of sentiment, as you may have observed, and I have been most shamefully treated over this wretched seal. But if all you tell me has been actually what has happened I have a sort of perverse inclination to forgive the man in spite of myself. The thing probably had been his mother's— or at any rate he believed so—and his giving up his little all to attain the object of his ridiculous faith, and distributing his goods among the poor people and all that—really it's worthy of an old martyr, if only it were done in the cause of a faith a little less stupid—though of course he thinks his is the only religion, as others do of theirs. But then"—Mrs. Mallett stiffened again—"there's not much to prove your theories, is there?"

Hewitt smiled. "Perhaps not," he said, "except that, to my mind at any rate, everything points to my explanation being the only possible one. The thing presented itself to you, from the beginning, as an attempt on the snuff-box you value so highly, and the possibility of the seal being the object aimed at never entered your mind. I saw it whole from the outside, and on thinking the thing over after our first interview I remembered Joanna Southcott. I think I am right."

"Well, if you are, as I said, I half believe I shall forgive the man. We will advertise if you like, telling him he has nothing to fear if he can give an explanation of his conduct consistent with what he calls his religious belief, absurd as it may be."

That night fell darker and foggier than the last. The advertisement went into the daily papers, but Reuben Penner nevers saw it. Late the next day a bargeman passing Old Swan Pier struck some large object with his boat-hook and brought it to the surface. It was the body of a drowned man, and it was afterwards identified as that of Reuben Penner, late greengrocer, of Hammersmith. How he came into the water there was nothing to show. There was no money nor any valuables found on the body, and there was a story of a large, heavy-faced man who had given a poor woman—a perfect stranger—a watch and chain and a handful of money down near Tower Hill on that foggy evening. But this again was only a story, not definitely authenticated. What was certain was that, tied securely round the dead man's neck with a cord, and gripped and crumpled tightly in his right hand, was a soddened piece of vellum paper, blank, but carrying an old red seal, of which the device was almost entirely rubbed and cracked away. Nobody at the inquest quite understood this.

ARTHUR MORRISON - A CONCISE BIBLIOGRAPHY

Tales of Mean Streets (1894)
Martin Hewitt, Investigator (1894)
Zig-Zags At The Zoo (1894)
The Chronicles of Martin Hewitt (1895)
The Adventures of Martin Hewitt (1896)
A Child of the Jago (1896)
The Dorrington Deed Box (1897)
To London Town (1899)
Cunning Murrell (1900)
The Hole in the Wall (1902)
The Red Triangle (1903)
The Green Eye of Goona (Released in the US as The Green Diamond) (1904)
Divers Vanities (1905)
Green Ginger (1909)
Fiddle O'Dreams And More (1933)

www.ingramcontent.com/pod-product-compliance
Lightning Source LLC
Chambersburg PA
CBHW071412170626
46811CB00003B/1375